HYGIENE
AND THE ASSASSIN

Amélie Nothomb

HYGIENE
AND THE ASSASSIN

*Translated from the French
by Alison Anderson*

Europa
editions

Europa Editions
116 East 16th Street
New York, N.Y. 10003
www.europaeditions.com
info@europaeditions.com

Translation by Alison Anderson
Original title: *Hygiène de l'assassin*
Translation copyright © 2010 by Europa Editions

Library of Congress Cataloging in Publication Data is available
ISBN 978-1-933372-77-8

Nothomb, Amélie
Hygiene and the Assassin

Ce livre a été publié avec l'aide du Ministère
de la Communauté française Belgique.

Book design by Emanuele Ragnisco
www.mekkanografici.com

Cover illustration by Emanuele Ragnisco

Prepress by Plan.ed
www.plan-ed.it

Printed in Canada

HYGIENE
AND THE ASSASSIN

When the imminent demise of the great writer Prétextat Tach became public knowledge—he was given two months to live—journalists the world over requested private interviews with the eighty-year-old gentleman. To be sure, he enjoyed considerable prestige; nevertheless, it was astonishing to see them flocking to his bedside, these emissaries from dailies as renowned as (we have taken the liberty of translating their names) *The Nanking Tattler* and *The Bangladesh Observer*. Thus, two months before his death, Monsieur Tach was given the opportunity to measure the extent of his celebrity.

His secretary set about making a drastic selection from among the various proposals: he eliminated all the solicitations from the foreign press, because the dying man spoke only French, and did not trust interpreters; he turned down all reporters of color, because with age the writer had begun to express racist views, which contrasted sharply with his most deeply held opinions—Tachian specialists were greatly discomfited, and interpreted this as a senile desire to cause a scandal; finally, the secretary politely discouraged requests from television networks, women's magazines, papers that were considered too political, and, above all, any medical journals that might have wanted to investigate how the great man had developed such a rare form of cancer.

It was not without a certain sense of pride that Monsieur Tach learned he was afflicted with the dread Elzenveiverplatz

Syndrome, more commonly referred to as "cartilage cancer," which the eponymous learned physician had individuated in Cayenne in the nineteenth century among a dozen or so convicts imprisoned for sexual crimes followed by homicide, and which had never been diagnosed since that time. Monsieur Tach viewed his diagnosis as a hitherto unhoped-for ennoblement: with his hairless, obese physique—that of a eunuch in every respect except for his voice—he dreaded dying of some stupid cardiovascular disease. Upon composing his epitaph, he was careful to mention the sublime name of the Teutonic doctor thanks to whom he would leave this world with a flourish.

Modern medicine was sincerely puzzled by the fact that this adipose, sedentary man had survived to the age of eighty-three. He was so fat that for years he had admitted to not being able to walk; he blatantly ignored any recommendations from nutritionists and had terrible eating habits. In addition, he smoked twenty Havana cigars a day. But his alcohol consumption was moderate, and he had practiced chastity since time immemorial: the doctors could find no alternative explanation for the sound functioning of a heart smothered in fat. For all that, his survival remained a mystery, like the origins of the syndrome that would bring an end to it.

Not a single newspaper the world over could help but be scandalized by the media coverage devoted to this upcoming death. Letters to the editor were largely devoted to reaffirming the papers' self-criticism. Thus, in keeping with the laws of modern news coverage, the features by the rare journalists who had been selected were eagerly anticipated.

Biographers were already hovering. Editors were arming their battalions. There were of course a number of intellectuals who wondered if the man's prodigious success was not overrated: had Prétextat Tach been truly innovative? Had he not simply been the ingenious heir to overlooked creators? They went on to support their thesis by citing authors with esoteric names, whose works they themselves had not read, a fact which enabled them to speak about them penetratingly.

All these factors helped to ensure that the man's dying moments would make an exceptional stir. No doubt about it: it was a resounding success.

The author, who had twenty-two novels to his name, lived on the ground floor of a modest building: he required accommodation where everything was on the same level, because he could only get around in a wheelchair. He lived alone, without any pets. Every day, a very brave nurse would come by at around five o'clock to bathe him. He could not have stood for anyone else to do his shopping, so he went himself to buy what he needed in the neighborhood stores. His secretary, Ernest Gravelin, lived four stories up, but as much as he could he avoided seeing him; he telephoned regularly, and Tach never missed an opportunity to begin their conversation by saying, "So sorry, my dear Ernest, I'm not dead yet."

Gravelin reminded those journalists who had been selected that the old man, basically, had a good heart: did he not give half his income every year to charitable organizations? And could this secret generosity not also be detected in some of the characters of his novels? "Of course he terrorizes us all, me to begin with, but I maintain that his mask of aggression is mere playfulness: he enjoys acting the placid, cruel fat man in order to hide his great sensitivity." His words did little to reassure the chroniclers who, in any case, had no desire to overcome their jealously guarded fear, for it gave them an aura of war correspondents.

The news of the writer's imminent death was reported on January 10. On the fourteenth a first journalist went to meet him. He entered the apartment: it was so dark that it took a moment before he was able to distinguish a corpulent figure in a wheelchair in the middle of the living room. The old man's lugubrious voice uttered no more than an inexpressive "Good morning, Monsieur," to put him at ease—which in fact only served to make the poor fellow more tense than ever.

"I am extremely pleased to meet you, Monsieur Tach. This is a great honor."

The tape recorder was switched on, eagerly awaiting the words of the silent old man.

"I beg your pardon, Monsieur Tach, would you mind if I switch on a light? I cannot see your face."

"It is ten o'clock in the morning, Monsieur; I do not switch on the lights at such a time. And besides, you will see me soon enough, once your eyes have adjusted to the darkness. So make the most of the respite you have been granted, and in the meantime you'll have to make do with my voice; it's the most beautiful thing about me."

"You do indeed have a very beautiful voice."

"Yes."

The silence weighed heavily upon the intruder, and he wrote in his notebook: "T.'s silence is caustic. Avoid as much as possible."

"Monsieur Tach, people the world over admire your determination to avoid being admitted to the hospital, despite all the doctors' orders. So the first question I must ask you is, how do you feel?"

"I feel just as I have felt for twenty years."

"In other words?"

"I do not feel much."

"Not much of what?"

"Not much."

"I understand."

"Then I admire you."

There was no irony in the sick man's implacably neutral voice. The journalist gave an awkward little laugh before continuing: "Monsieur Tach, with a man like yourself, I won't waste time with the circumlocutions common to my profession. So, if you'll allow me, I'll ask you outright: what might be the thoughts and moods of a great writer who knows he is going to die?"

Silence. A sigh.

"I don't know, my good man."

"You don't know?"

"If I knew what I was thinking, I suppose I would never have become a writer."

"You mean that you write in order to find out what you are thinking?"

"It's a possibility. I'm not really sure anymore, it's been such a long time since I've written anything."

"What? But your last novel came out less than two years ago . . ."

"Emptying my drawers, my good man. There is enough material in my drawers for a new novel by me to be published every year for a full decade after my death."

"That's extraordinary! When did you stop writing?"

"At the age of fifty-nine."

"Then that means that all the novels that have come out in the last twenty-four years . . . you were emptying your drawers?"

"You have done your math."

"How old were you when you began to write?"

"That would be hard to say: I began, then stopped, several times. The first time, I was six years old, and I wrote tragedies."

"Tragedies at the age of six?"

"Yes, and in verse. Ludicrous. I stopped when I was seven. At the age of nine I had a relapse, which earned me a few elegies, again in verse. I had nothing but scorn for prose."

"That's astonishing, coming from one of the greatest prose writers of our era."

"At the age of eleven I stopped again, and did not write another line until I was eighteen."

The journalist wrote in his notebook: "T. does not respond to compliments."

"And then?"

"I started writing again. To begin with I wrote fairly little, then more and more. By the age of twenty-three I had hit my cruising speed, and maintained it for the next thirty-six years."

"What do you mean by 'cruising speed'?"

"That I did nothing else. I wrote, nonstop; apart from eating, smoking, and sleeping, I had no other activity."

"You never went out?"

"Only when forced to."

"In fact, no one has ever found out what you did during the war."

"Neither have I."

"How do you expect me to believe that?"

"It's the truth. From the age of twenty-three to the age of fifty-nine, all my days were alike. I have a long, homogeneous memory of those thirty-six years, which were virtually devoid of chronology. I got up to write and went to bed when I had finished writing."

"But, after all, you must have gone through the war like everyone. For example, how did you feed yourself?"

The journalist knew he had touched upon one of the fat man's major preoccupations.

"Yes, I do recall eating badly during those years."

"So you see!"

"I did not suffer. In those days I was a glutton, not a gourmet. And I had an extraordinary reserve of cigars."

"When did you become a gourmet?"

"When I stopped writing. Before that, I did not have time."

"And why did you stop writing?"

"On the day of my fifty-ninth birthday I felt it was all over."

"What made you feel that way?"

"I don't know. It simply came on, like menopause. I left one novel unfinished. That's fine: in a successful career, you must always have one unfinished novel if you are to be taken seriously. Otherwise, they think you're a third-rate writer."

"So you spent thirty-six years writing continuously, and from one day to the next—not another line?"

"Correct."

"What have you been doing for the last twenty-four years, then?"

"I told you, I became a gourmet."

"Full time?"

"Let's say, rather, full capacity."

"And other than that?"

"It takes time, you know. Other than that, almost nothing. I reread some classics. Ah yes, I forgot, I bought a television."

"What, you like television?"

"Commercials, only commercials. I love them."

"Nothing else?"

"No, I don't like television, other than commercials."

"This is extraordinary: so you have spent the last twenty-four years eating and watching television?"

"No, I have also been sleeping and smoking. And reading a bit."

"And yet we have been hearing about you constantly."

"That's the fault of my excellent secretary, Ernest Gravelin. He's the one who empties out my drawers, meets my publishers, fuels my legend, and, above all, brings me the latest doctors' theories—they all hope to put me on a diet."

"In vain."

"Fortunately. It would have been really too silly to deprive me because, at the end of the day, the origin of my cancer is not nutritional."

"What is the origin of your cancer?"

"It's mysterious, but not nutritional. According to Elzenveiverplatz"—(here the fat man took great delight in articu-

lating the name),—"it seems to be the result of a genetic accident, programmed before my birth. Therefore, I was quite right
to eat anything and everything."

"So you were already doomed at birth?"

"Yes, Monsieur, like a true tragic hero. And to think there
are people who still talk about human freedom."

"But you were granted a reprieve of eighty-three years all the
same."

"A reprieve, precisely."

"But you won't deny that during those eighty-three years
you have been free? For example, you could very well have
chosen not to write . . ."

"Might you by any chance be reproaching me for having
written?"

"That's not what I meant."

"Ah. A pity, I was beginning to have some respect for you."

"But you don't regret having written?"

"Regret? I am incapable of regret. Would you like a toffee?"

"No, thank you."

The novelist shoved a caramel in his mouth and chewed it
noisily.

"Monsieur Tach, are you afraid of death?"

"Not at all. Death must not be a very big change. I do, however, have a fear of pain. I've acquired a stockpile of morphine,
which I can inject myself. Thanks to this measure, I'm no longer
afraid."

"Do you believe in life after death?"

"No."

"So, do you believe that death is annihilation?"

"How can you annihilate something that has already been
annihilated?"

"That's a terrible answer."

"It isn't an answer."

"I see."

"Good for you."

"Well, what I meant was . . ." The journalist attempted to come up with something he might have meant to say if not for being thrown off by a difficulty in putting his words together. ". . . a novelist is a person who asks questions, not one who answers them."

Silence of the dead.

"Well, that's not exactly what I meant . . ."

"No? Pity. I was just beginning to think that was rather good."

"And may we talk about your oeuvre, now?"

"If you insist."

"You don't like to talk about it, do you?"

"I can't hide a thing from you."

"Like all great writers, you are very modest when it comes to your work."

"Modest, me? You must be mistaken."

"You seem to enjoy underestimating your own worth. Why do you deny that you are modest?"

"Because, Monsieur, I am not."

"Then why are you so reluctant to talk about your novels?"

"Because there is no point in talking about a novel."

"But it's fascinating to hear a writer talk about his creation, to hear him say how and why he writes, and what he writes against."

"If a writer manages to be fascinating about his own novels, then there are only two possibilities: either he is merely voicing out loud what he wrote in his book, and he is a parrot; or he is explaining interesting things that he didn't discuss in his book, in which case the book in question is a failure, since it does not live up to its claims."

"But still, any number of great writers have been able to talk about their work and avoid such pitfalls."

"You are contradicting yourself: two minutes ago you said

that all great writers were extremely modest when it came to their work."

"But you can talk about a work and still preserve its mystery."

"Oh, indeed? Have you ever tried?"

"No, but I'm not a writer."

"Then what makes you think you are entitled to come out with such rubbish?"

"You are not the first writer I have ever interviewed."

"Might you by any chance be comparing me to those scribblers you normally interview?"

"They are not scribblers!"

"If they can discuss their oeuvre and be fascinating and modest at the same time, there can be no doubt that they are scribblers. How can a writer possibly be modest? It is the most immodest profession on earth: whether it's the style, the ideas, the story, the research, writers never talk about anything but themselves and, what's more, with words. Painters and musicians also talk about themselves, but with a language that is substantially less crude than our own. No, Monsieur, writers are obscene; if they were not, they would be accountants, or train conductors, or telephone operators; they would be respectable."

"That's as may be. How do you explain the fact that you personally are so modest?"

"What on earth are you going on about?"

"Well, yes. For sixty years you have been a fully fledged writer, and this is your first interview. You are never featured in the press, you do not belong to any literary or nonliterary circles, and by all appearances, you only leave this apartment to do your shopping. You are not even known to have any friends. If that is not modesty, what is it?"

"Have your eyes adjusted to the darkness? Can you make out my face now?"

"Yes, vaguely."

"Well, good for you. Let me tell you, sir, that if I were handsome, I would not live as a recluse. In fact, if I had been handsome, I would never have become a writer. I would have been an adventurer, or a slave trader, or a barman, or a fortune hunter."

"So are you saying there is a connection between your looks and your vocation?"

"It is not a vocation. It came to me the day I became aware of my ugliness."

"And when was that?"

"I was very young. I have always been ugly."

"You're not that ugly."

"You, at least, are tactful."

"Well, you're fat, but you're not ugly."

"What more do you want? Four chins, piggy eyes, a nose like a spud, no more hair on my head than on my cheeks, my neck is one roll of fat upon the other, my jowls droop—and, out of consideration for you, I have only described my face."

"Have you always been this fat?"

"At the age of eighteen, I was already like this—you can say obese, it doesn't bother me."

"Yes, obese, but we can still look at you without trembling."

"I'll grant you that I could have been even more repugnant: I might have had a blotchy face, covered in warts . . ."

"As it is, you have very nice skin, it's white and smooth, I can tell it must be very soft to the touch."

"A eunuch's complexion, my good man. There's something almost grotesque about having such skin on my face, particularly on a chubby, clean-shaven face: in fact, my head resembles a fine pair of smooth, soft buttocks. My head inspires laughter rather than disgust, although there are times I would have preferred to inspire disgust. It's more invigorating."

"I would never have imagined that you suffer from your looks."

"I don't suffer. Suffering is for other people, for those who see me. I don't see myself. I never look at myself in the mirror. I would suffer if I had chosen another life; but for the life I lead, this body suits me fine."

"Would you have preferred another life?"

"I don't know. Sometimes I think that all lives are equal. One thing is sure, and that is that I have no regrets. If I were eighteen years old now, with the same body, I would start all over again, I would reproduce exactly the same life, insofar as you can say I've had a life."

"Isn't writing a life?"

"I'm not in a good position to answer that question. I've never done anything else."

"You've had twenty-two novels published, and according to what you have told me, there will be even more. Among the host of characters who inhabit your immense oeuvre, is there one in particular who resembles you more than others?"

"Not a one."

"Really? Let me tell you something: there is one of your characters who seems to me to be your exact double."

"Ah."

"Yes, the mysterious wax vendor, in *Crucifixion Made Easy.*"

"The wax vendor? What an absurd idea."

"I'll tell you why: when he's the one speaking, you always write 'crucifiction.'"

"So?"

"He's no fool. He knows that it's a fiction."

"And so does the reader. But that doesn't mean he resembles me."

"And this mania of his, making wax masks of the faces of the crucified—that's you, isn't it?"

"I've never made wax masks of crucified people, I assure you."

"No, of course not, but it's a metaphor for what you do."

"What do you know about metaphors, young man?"

"But . . . I know what everyone knows."

"An excellent reply. People don't know a thing about metaphors. It's a word that sells well, because it sounds classy. 'Metaphor': even the most illiterate person can tell it comes from Greek. Incredibly chic, these phony etymologies, and absolutely phony: when you are familiar with the dreadful polysemy of the preposition *meta* and the polyvalent neutrality of the verb *phero*, if you're at all in good faith you should logically conclude that the word 'metaphor' doesn't mean a thing. Besides, when you hear how people use and abuse it, you come to exactly the same conclusion."

"What do you mean?"

"Precisely what I said. I don't use metaphors to express myself, now do I?"

"But the wax casts?"

"The wax casts are wax casts, sir."

"It's my turn to be disappointed, Monsieur Tach, because if you exclude the metaphorical interpretation, all that's left of your work is bad taste."

"Well, there are all sorts of bad taste: there is healthy, regenerative bad taste, which consists in creating horrible things for salubrious, purgative, robust, male purposes, like a good well-controlled binge of vomiting, and then there's the other bad taste—it is apostolic, offended by such elegant barfing, and in need of a waterproof diving suit in order to make its way through. This particular frogman is the metaphor that enables the relieved maker of metaphors to exclaim, 'I went from one end of Tach to the other, and I didn't get dirty!'"

"But that, too, is a metaphor."

"Obviously: I try to crush metaphors with their own weapons. If I had wanted to play the Messiah, if I had had to rouse the rabble, I would have cried out, 'Conscripts, come and enlist in my redemptive mission; let us metaphorize our metaphors, let us amalgamate them, beat them until they're stiff, let's make them into a soufflé and let that soufflé puff up, a gorgeous expansion, getting bigger and bigger until it explodes, conscripts, then subsides and collapses and disappoints all the guests, to our utmost delight!"

"A writer who hates metaphors is as absurd as a banker who hates money."

"I am sure that great bankers hate money. There's nothing absurd about it, on the contrary."

"Words, however—you do love words?"

"Oh, I adore words, but there's no comparison. Words are a fine substance, sacred ingredients."

"So metaphors are a form of cooking—and you do like cooking."

"No, Monsieur, metaphors are not cooking—syntax is cooking. Metaphors are bad faith; it's like biting into a tomato and asserting that the tomato tastes like honey, and then eating honey and saying it tastes like ginger, then chewing on ginger and saying the ginger tastes like sarsaparilla, and at that point . . ."

"Yes, I understand, sir, you needn't go on."

"No, you don't understand: to make you understand what a metaphor really is, I would have to go on playing this little game for hours, because metaphorians never stop, they will go on playing until some well-intentioned person comes along to smash their face in."

"And are you that well-intentioned person?"

"No. I've always been a little too soft and too kind."

"Kind, you?"

"Terribly. I know of no one as kind as I am. And such kindness is terrifying, because I am never kind out of mere kindness, but only out of weariness and, above all, a fear of exasperation. I get exasperated very easily, and I find exasperation very hard to take, so I avoid it like the plague."

"You scorn kindness, in other words?"

"You haven't understood a thing of what I'm trying to tell you. I admire kindness when it is truly founded on kindness or love. But how many people do you know who actually practice that form of kindness? In the vast majority of cases, when human beings are kind it is in order to be left alone."

"Granted. But that still doesn't explain why the wax vendor was making casts of the faces of the crucified."

"And why shouldn't he? Every trade has its own merits. You're a journalist, are you not? Have I asked you why you're a journalist?"

"Go right ahead. I'm a journalist because there's a demand, because people are interested in my articles, because they're buying them from me, and because it enables me to communicate information."

"In your shoes, I wouldn't brag about it."

"But Monsieur Tach, I have to make a living!"

"Do you think so?"

"That's what you're doing, no?"

"That remains to be seen."

"It's what your wax vendor does, in any case."

"You really do have a thing about this old wax vendor, don't you? Why does he make casts of the crucified? For reasons, I suppose, directly opposed to your own: because there is no demand, because people aren't interested, because no one buys his casts, and because it doesn't enable him to communicate information."

"An expression of the absurd, maybe?"

"It's no more absurd than what you do, if you want my opinion—but I'm not sure you do."

"Of course I do, I'm a journalist."

"Precisely."

"Why do you feel such hostility toward journalists?"

"Not toward journalists, toward you."

"What have I done to deserve it?"

"This is too much. Here you have been insulting me, treating me as a metaphorian, accusing me of bad taste, inferring that I was not 'so' ugly, importuning the wax vendor and now, to take the cake, you claim to understand me."

"But . . . what am I supposed to say?"

"That's your profession, not mine. When one is as stupid as you are, he ought not to harangue Prétextat Tach."

"You yourself gave me permission."

"I most certainly did not. It was that idiot of a secretary, Gravelin, and he has no talent for discernment."

"Earlier, you said he was an excellent man."

"That doesn't preclude stupidity."

"Come now, Monsieur Tach, don't make yourself more disagreeable than you already are."

"You vulgar so-and-so! Leave here at once!"

"But . . . the interview has only just begun!"

"It has lasted far too long already, you ill-mannered lout! Get out of here! And tell your colleagues to show some respect for Prétextat Tach!"

The journalist hurried away, his tail between his legs.

His colleagues were having a drink at the café across the street and hadn't expected to see him come out so soon; they waved to him. The poor fellow was green, and he collapsed in their midst.

Once he'd ordered a triple egg flip, he found the strength to relate his misadventure. His fear meant he was giving off a terrible smell, which must not have been unlike that of Jonah emerging from his cetacean sojourn. His companions found it off-putting. Was he aware of his fustiness? He himself evoked Jonah: "The belly of the whale! I assure you, it was all there! Dark, ugly, frightening, claustrophobic . . ."

"Did it stink?" ventured a colleague.

"That was about the only thing that was missing. But the man himself—like a slimy intestine! Smooth as a liver, as blown up as his belly must be. Perfidious as a spleen, and as bitter as a gallbladder! Just the way he looked at me, I felt as if he were digesting me, dissolving me in the juices of his totalitarian metabolism!"

"Go on, you're exaggerating!"

"On the contrary, I'll never find words strong enough. If you could have seen how angry he was at the end! I've never seen such terrifying anger: it was both sudden and perfectly controlled. You'd expect a lard-ass like him to go red, swell up, have trouble breathing, and sweat like a pig. Not at all, the only thing that equaled the suddenness of his anger was his coldness. If you could have heard his voice when he told me to get out! It was just how I imagined a Chinese emperor would speak when ordering an immediate beheading."

"In any case, he gave you the opportunity to play the hero."

"Do you think so? I've never felt so pathetic."

He gulped down his egg flip and burst into tears.

"Go on, this won't be the first time anyone's taken a journalist for an idiot."

"It's true, I've heard worse. But there was just something about the way he said it, his smooth face icy with scorn: it was very convincing."

"Can you let us hear the recording?"

In a religious silence, the tape recorder unreeled its truth, which was bound to be partial, because it had been amputated of the darkness, the placid features, the huge inexpressive hands, the general immobility, and everything which had contributed to make the poor journalist reek with fear. When they had finished listening, his colleagues, cruel as only humans can be, could not help but think the novelist was right: they admired him, and each one had to put in his two cents and lecture the victim.

"Sorry old boy, but you asked for it! The way you talked about literature with him—as if from a school book. I totally understand his reaction."

"Why did you want to identify him with one of his characters? What a simplistic idea."

"And those biographical questions, nobody cares about that. Haven't you read Proust, *Contre Sainte-Beuve?*"

"You really screwed up, saying that you're used to interviewing writers."

"How tactless can you get, saying he's not 'so' ugly! Don't you have any manners, you pitiful old thing?"

"And what about the metaphor! He really got you there. I don't mean to be hurtful, but you deserved it."

"Honestly, how can you talk about the absurd with a genius like Tach? It's pure slapstick."

"In any case, one thing is patently clear about this botched interview of yours: this guy is amazing! So intelligent!"

"So eloquent!"

"So much finesse for a fat man!"

"So nasty and yet so concise!"

"But you do agree, at least, that he is nasty?" cried the unfortunate fellow, clinging to this notion as if it were his last hope.

"Not nasty enough, if you want my opinion."

"I think he was even quite good-natured with you."

"And funny. When you—forgive me—were stupid enough to tell him you understood, he could easily, in all fairness, have come out with a scathing insult. But he merely showed his sense of humor—completely tongue-in-cheek, and you couldn't even see it."

"*Margaritas ante porcos.*"

They were going for the jugular. The victim ordered another triple egg flip.

As for Prétextat Tach, he preferred Brandy Alexanders. He

did not drink a great deal, but when he wanted to imbibe a little something, it was always a Brandy Alexander. He insisted on preparing it himself, because he did not trust other people's proportions. Luxuriating in spite, the intransigent fat man was wont to repeat an adage that he himself had coined: "You can measure an individual's bad faith by the way he mixes a Brandy Alexander."

If one were to apply this axiom to Tach himself, one would be forced to concur that he was the very incarnation of good faith. A single sip of his Brandy Alexander would suffice to defeat the champion of any raw egg or condensed milk ingestion contest. The novelist could digest an entire tankard without a flicker of indisposition. When Gravelin marveled at his employer's prowess, the fat man replied, "I am the Mithridates of Brandy Alexanders."

"But can we even still call it a Brandy Alexander?"

"It is the quintessence of Brandy Alexanders, and the rabble will never know anything but unworthy dilutions thereof."

To such august declarations, there is nothing more to add.

"Monsieur Tach, before anything else, on behalf of my entire profession I would like to apologize for what happened yesterday."

"What is supposed to have happened yesterday?"

"Well, that journalist dishonored us, bothering you the way he did."

"Ah yes, I remember. A very nice boy. When will I see him again?"

"Never again, rest assured. You might like to know that he's sick as a dog today."

"Poor boy! What happened?"

"Too many egg flips."

"I've always known that egg flips can play dirty tricks on you. If I had been aware of his taste for such invigorating beverages, I would have mixed him a good Brandy Alexander, there's nothing like it for the metabolism. Would you like a Brandy Alexander, young man?"

"Never while I'm on duty, thank you."

The journalist failed to notice the intensely suspicious gaze that his refusal inspired.

"Monsieur Tach, you must not be angry with our colleague over what happened yesterday. There are not many journalists who have been properly prepared to meet individuals like yourself . . ."

"That's all we need. Train good people so they can meet me! You could call such a discipline 'The art of dealing with geniuses'! How dreadful!"

"You think so? May I conclude that you won't hold it against my colleague? Thank you for your understanding."

"Have you come here to talk about your colleague, or to talk about me?"

"About you, of course; this was just by way of introduction."

"What a pity. Dear Lord, the prospect is so distressing that I need a Brandy Alexander. I hope you don't mind waiting a moment—it's your fault, after all, you shouldn't have mentioned Brandy Alexanders, you've made me want one with all your carrying on."

"But I never said anything about Brandy Alexanders!"

"Don't start off on the wrong foot, young man. I cannot stand bad faith. You still don't want to taste my beverage?"

He did not realize that Tach was offering him his last chance, and he let it slip by. Shrugging his huge shoulders, the novelist wheeled his chair over toward a sort of coffin, then raised the lid, revealing bottles, cans of food, and tankards.

"This is a Merovingian coffin," explained the fat man, "that I've converted into a bar."

He took hold of one of three big metal goblets, poured a generous dose of crème de cacao, and then some brandy. He gave the journalist a cunning glance.

"And now, you're going to learn the chef's secret. The common of mortals adds a final third of heavy cream. I think that's a bit too rich, so I've replaced the cream by an equivalent amount of . . ."—(he grabbed hold of one on the cans)—"sweet condensed milk." (And went on to illustrate his words with his gesture.)

"But that must be disgustingly rich!" said the journalist, sinking ever deeper.

"This year, we're having a mild winter. When it's cold, I add a big dollop of melted butter to my Brandy Alexander."

"I beg your pardon?"

"Yes. Condensed milk does not contain as much fat as cream, so you have to make up for it. In fact, as it is still only January

15, theoretically I am entitled to add some butter, but to do so I would have to go into the kitchen and leave you alone, and that would be ill-mannered. So I will do without the butter."

"Please, I beg you, don't deprive yourself for my sake."

"No, never mind. In honor of the ultimatum that expires this evening, I shall do without butter."

"Do you feel directly concerned by the Gulf crisis?"

"So concerned that I am not adding butter to my Brandy Alexander."

"Do you follow the news on television?"

"Between two commercial breaks, I sometimes subject myself to the news."

"What do you think of the Gulf crisis?"

"Nothing."

"You still think nothing?"

"Nothing."

"You're completely indifferent to it?"

"Not at all. But what I might think about it is irrelevant. You shouldn't ask a fat man for his opinion on this crisis. I am neither a general, nor a pacifist, nor a gas station attendant, nor an Iraqi. However, if you ask me about Brandy Alexanders, I shall be brilliant."

To conclude his flight of eloquence, the novelist raised the tankard to his lips and quaffed a few gluttonous gulps.

"Why do you drink from a metal container?"

"I don't like transparency. That is also one of the reasons why I am so fat: I don't like for people to see through me."

"Speaking of which, Monsieur Tach, I would like to ask you something that all the journalists are burning to ask, but have never dared."

"How much I weigh?"

"No, what you eat. We know that food is a very important part of your life. Gastronomy, and its natural consequence, digestion, are at the heart of some of your recent novels, such as *An Apology for Dyspepsia*, a work which, to me, seems to contain a condensed version of your metaphysical concerns."

"Exactly. I consider metaphysics to be the best form of expression for the metabolism. Along the same line, since one's metabolism can be divided into anabolism and catabolism, I have split metaphysics into anaphysics and cataphysics. This should not be seen as a dualist tension, but as two obligatory and, more inconveniently, simultaneous phases of a thought process devoted to triviality."

"Is this not also an allusion to Jarry and pataphysics?"

"No, monsieur. *I* am a serious writer," answered the old man icily, before imbibing another swallow of Brandy Alexander.

"So, Monsieur Tach, if you please, would you be so kind as to outline for me the various digestive stages in a typical day of your life?"

There was a solemn silence, while the novelist seemed to be thinking. Then he began to speak, in a grave tone of voice, as if he were unveiling some secret dogma.

"In the morning, I wake up at around eight o'clock. To begin with, I go to the toilet to empty my bladder and my intestines. Would you like any details?"

"No, I think that should be enough."

"So much the better, because while it is an indispensable stage in the digestive process, it is absolutely disgusting, that you may believe."

"I'll take your word for it."

"Blessed are they who have not seen and yet have believed. After that, I powder myself, then I get dressed."

"Do you always wear this dressing gown?"

"Yes, except when I go out shopping."

"Does your handicap not make it difficult to get around?"

"I've had time to get used to it. Then I go into the kitchen and make my breakfast. In the old days, when I spent my time writing, I didn't cook, and I ate coarse meals, such as cold tripe . . ."

"Cold tripe in the morning?"

"I can see why you might be surprised. You must realize that in those days, writing was virtually my sole preoccupation. But nowadays I would find it repulsive to eat cold tripe in the morning. For twenty years I have been in the habit of browning it in goose fat for half an hour."

"Tripe in goose fat for breakfast?"

"It's excellent."

"And you have a Brandy Alexander with that?"

"No, never when I eat. Back in the days when I was writing, I drank strong coffee. Nowadays I prefer eggnog. After that, I go out shopping and spend my morning cooking up a refined dish for lunch: fritters of brain, kidneys *en daube* . . ."

"And complicated desserts?"

"Rarely. I drink only sweet things, so I don't really feel like dessert. The occasional toffee between meals. When I was young, I preferred Scottish toffees, which are exceptionally hard. Alas, with age, I now have to make do with soft toffees, which are excellent nonetheless. I venture to claim that nothing can equal the voluptuous sensation of being bogged down that is concomitant with the paralysis of one's jaws caused by chewing English toffees . . . Do write down what I just said, I think it rings rather well."

"There's no need, it's all being recorded."

"What? But that's dishonest! I can't say anything foolish, in other words?"

"You never say anything foolish, monsieur Tach."

"You are as flattering as a sycophant, Monsieur."

"Please, do go on with your digestive stations of the Cross."

"My digestive stations of the Cross? That's a good one. You didn't steal it from one of my novels by any chance?"

"No, I made it up."

"That would surprise me. I would swear it was Prétextat Tach. There was a time when I knew my works by heart . . . Alas, we are as old as our memory, don't you agree? And it's not the arteries, as some imbeciles would have it. Let's see, 'digestive stations of the Cross,' where did I write that?"

"Monsieur Tach, even if you had written it, I would be just as deserving for saying it, given that—"

The journalist came to a sudden stop, biting his lips.

"—given that you've never read a thing I've written, have you? Thank you, young man, that's all I wanted to know. Who are you to believe such boundless twaddle? Do you honestly think I would ever make up such a flashy, mediocre expression as 'digestive stations of the Cross'? It's just about worthy of a second-rate theologian like yourself. Well, I can see with a somewhat senile sense of relief that the literary world has not changed: it is still the triumph of those who pretend to have read What's-his-name. However, even that is no longer an achievement, for nowadays you can buy so-called study guides that enable illiterate people to talk about great authors with every appearance of a person of average culture. And this is where you are mistaken: I consider the fact that someone has not read me to be most deserving. I would have warm admiration for a journalist who came to interview me without even knowing who I am, and who would not hide his ignorance. But if you know nothing of me except what amounts to an instant powdered milkshake—can you imagine anything more mediocre?"

"Try to understand. Today is the fifteenth, and the news about your cancer was announced on the tenth. You have already published twenty-two major novels, it would have been impossible to read them in so little time, particularly in these turbulent days when we are all focused on the latest news from the Middle East."

"The Gulf crisis is more interesting than my corpse, I'll grant you that. But the time you spent cramming with the help of those study guides would have been better spent reading even just ten pages from one of my twenty-two books."

"I have something to confess."

"There is no need, I understand: you tried, and you gave up before you had even reached page 10, is that it? I guessed as much, the moment I saw you. I can recognize instantaneously the people who have read me: you can see it on their face. But you looked neither upset, nor bright, nor fat, nor thin, nor ecstatic: you looked healthy. So you haven't read any more of me than your colleague from yesterday. And that is why, in spite of everything, I still find you somewhat to my liking. All the more so in that you gave up before page 10: that is proof of a strength of character I have never been capable of. Moreover, your attempt to confess—superfluous—does you credit. In fact, I would have disliked you immensely if you had well and truly read me, and were just as I see you now. But that is enough laughable conjecture. We were talking about my digestion, if my memory serves me correctly?"

"That's right. Talking about toffees, to be exact."

"Well, when I have finished lunch, I head for the smoking room. This is one of the high points of the day. I can only tolerate your interviews in the morning, because in the afternoon, I smoke until five o'clock."

"Why five o'clock?"

"At five o'clock this stupid nurse arrives, who thinks it's useful to bathe me from head to toe: yet another one of Gravelin's ideas. A daily bath, can you imagine? *Vanitas vanitatum sed omnia vanitas.* So I take my revenge however I can, I find a way to stink as much as I can, so as to inconvenience that innocent young thing. I garnish my lunch with entire heads of garlic, I invent all sorts of circulatory ailments, and then I smoke like a Turk until the intrusion of my washerwoman."

He gave a hideous laugh.

"Don't tell me you smoke like that with the sole intention of asphyxiating the unfortunate woman?"

"That would be reason enough, but the truth is that I adore

smoking cigars. If I didn't choose to smoke at that time, there would be nothing pernicious about the activity—I insist on the word 'activity', because for me, smoking is an activity in its own right, and I can tolerate no visits or distractions while I'm smoking."

"This is very interesting, Monsieur Tach, but let's not get off the subject: your cigars have nothing to do with your digestion."

"You don't think so? I'm not so sure. Well, if it doesn't interest you . . . And my bath, are you interested in that?"

"No, unless you eat the soap or drink the bath water."

"Can you imagine, that bitch has me get naked, then she scrubs my spare tires, and showers my hindquarters? I'm sure it gives her an orgasm, just to be soaking a naked, hairless, crippled fat man. Those nurses are all obsessed. That's why they go into such a filthy profession."

"Monsieur Tach, I believe we are getting off the subject again . . ."

"I don't agree. This daily episode is so perverse that it upsets my digestion. Can you imagine! I'm all alone, humiliated, monstrously fat, and as naked as a worm in the bathwater, in the presence of this clothed creature who undresses me every day, wearing her hypocritically professional expression to hide the fact that she's wetting her underpants—if the bitch is even wearing any—and when she goes back to the hospital, I'm sure she shares all the details with her girlfriends—they're all bitches, too—and maybe they even—"

"Monsieur Tach, please!"

"This will teach you to record me, young man! If you took notes like any honest journalist, you could censor the senile horrors I'm sharing with you. With your machine, however, there is no way you can sort out my pearls from my filthy rubbish."

"And once the nurse has left?"

"She's left already? You don't waste time. Once she's left, it's already six o'clock or later. That bitch has gotten me in my pajamas, like a baby you bathe and wrap up in his rompers before giving him his last bottle. By then I feel so infantile that I play."

"You play? What do you play?"

"Anything. I drive around in my wheelchair, I set up a slalom, I play darts—look at the wall behind you, you'll see the damage—or else, supreme delight, I tear out the bad pages in classic novels."

"What?"

"Yes, I expurgate. *La Princesse de Clèves*, for example: it's an excellent novel, but it's far too long. I don't suppose you have read it, so I recommend the version I have taken the pains to abridge: a quintessential masterpiece."

"Monsieur Tach, what would you say if, three centuries from now, someone tore the pages deemed superfluous from your novels?"

"I challenge you to find even one superfluous page in my books."

"Madame de La Fayette would have told you the same thing."

"You're not going to compare me to that schoolgirl, are you?"

"Really, Monsieur Tach . . ."

"Would you like to know my secret dream? An auto-da-fé. A fine auto-da-fé of my entire work! That's shut you up, hasn't it?"

"Fine. And after your entertainment?"

"You are obsessed with food, I swear! The moment I talk about anything else, you get me onto the subject of food again."

"I am not obsessed, but since we started on that subject, we have to see it through to the end."

"You're not obsessed? You disappoint me, young man. So let's talk about food, since it doesn't obsess you. When I've finish expurgating, and have had a good round of darts, and slalomed and played nicely, when these educational activities have made me forget the horrors of my bath, I switch on the television, the way little children do, watching their idiotic programs before they have their pablum or their alphabet soup. At that time of day, it's very interesting. There are endless amounts of commercials, primarily about food. I channel surf in order to put together the longest sequence of commercials on earth: with the sixteen European channels, it is perfectly feasible, if you surf intelligently, to get a full half-hour of uninterrupted commercials. It's a marvelous multilingual opera: Dutch shampoo, Italian cookies, German organic washing powder, French butter, and so on. What a treat. When the programs get too inane, I switch off the television. I've worked up an appetite after all the hundreds of commercials I've seen, so I set about making some food. You're pleased, aren't you? You should have seen your face, when I pretended to be getting off the subject again. Rest assured, you'll get your scoop. In the evening I have a fairly light meal. I'm perfectly happy with cold dishes, such as *rillettes*, solidified fat, raw bacon, the oil from a tin of sardines—I don't like the sardines very much, but they do flavor the oil, so I throw out the sardines and save the juice, and drink it on its own. . . Good heavens, what's wrong?"

"Nothing. Please continue."

"You don't look very well, I assure you. Along with that I heat up a very fatty bouillon, prepared ahead of time: for hours, I boil cheese rind, pigs' trotters, chicken rumps, marrowbones, and a carrot. I add a ladleful of lard, remove the carrot, and let it cool for twenty-four hours. In fact, I like to drink the bouillon when it's cold, when the fat has hardened into a crust that leaves my lips glistening. But don't worry, I don't waste a thing, don't go thinking that I throw out all that delicate meat. After I've boiled it for a long time, the meat gains in unctuousness what it's lost in juice: the chicken rumps are a real treat, the yellow fat takes on a lovely spongy texture . . . What is the matter?"

"I . . . I don't know. Claustrophobia, perhaps. Could we open a window?"

"Open a window, on January 15? Don't even think about it. The oxygen would kill you. No, I know what you need."

"Please let me go out for a moment."

"It's out of the question, stay where it's warm. I'm going to make you one of my very own Brandy Alexanders, with melted butter."

Upon hearing this, the journalist's livid complexion turned bright green: he went off at a run, bent double, his hand on his mouth.

Tach wheeled at full tilt to the window overlooking the street, and had the intense satisfaction of contemplating the unfortunate man on his knees, retching, overwhelmed.

The fat man muttered into his four chins, jubilant, "When you have a delicate constitution, you don't go trying to measure up to Prétextat Tach!"

Hidden behind the net curtain, he could indulge in the delight of seeing without being seen, and he witnessed two men running out of the café across the street, to hurry over to their colleague who, his guts now empty, lay on the sidewalk next to his tape recorder, which he had not switched off: he had recorded the sound of his own vomiting.

The journalist had collapsed on the bench in the bistro and was recovering as best he could. He said again and again, his expression bleak, "No more food . . . I don't ever want to eat again . . ."

They got him to drink a little bit of lukewarm water that he eyed suspiciously. His colleagues wanted to listen to the tape; he intervened.

"Not in my presence, I beg you."

They called the victim's wife, and she came to collect him with her car. Once he had left, they could at last switch on the tape recorder. The writer's words aroused disgust, laughter, and enthusiasm.

"This guy is a gold mine. He's what I'd call a force of nature."

"He's wonderfully abject."

"At least he doesn't subscribe to some sort of soft ideology."

"Or lite ideology!"

"There's something about the way he throws his adversary."

"He's really good at it. Our friend, on the other hand, fell into every trap."

"I don't like to speak badly about someone who's not here, but what was he thinking, asking him all those questions about food! I can see why the fat man wouldn't put up with it. When you have the opportunity to question such a genius, you don't go talking about food."

The journalists were secretly delighted that they hadn't gone first or second. If they had been completely honest with themselves, they would have admitted that, in their unfortunate predecessors' shoes, they would have brought up the same subjects—stupid to be sure, but mandatory—and they were delighted that as a result they would not have to do the dirty work: they could put on their best face, and make the most of it, although this did not prevent them from having a bit of a laugh at the expense of the victims.

So, on that terrible day when the entire world trembled at the prospect of imminent war, an adipose, paralytic, unarmed old man had managed to draw the attention of a handful of media priests away from the Persian Gulf. There was even one who, on that night where all were sleepless, went to bed on an empty stomach and slept the heavy, exhausting sleep of those who suffer from liver complaints, with nary a thought for those about to die.

Tach was milking the innate potential of disgust for all it was worth. Fat was his napalm, Brandy Alexanders were his chemical weapon. That evening, he rubbed his hands together, a gleeful strategist.

S o, has the war started?"

"Not yet, Monsieur Tach."

"It is going to start, isn't it?"

"Listening to you, anyone would think you hope it will."

"I can't stand it when promises are not kept. A bunch of goons promised us a war for January 15 at midnight. It's the six-teenth and nothing has happened. Who do they take us for? Bil-lions of television viewers are anxiously waiting."

"Are you in favor of this war, Monsieur Tach?"

"You mean do I love war! Unthinkable! How can anyone love war? What a ridiculous, pointless question. Do you know anyone who loves war? Why don't you ask me if I have napalm for breakfast, while you're at it?"

"As regards your eating habits, I think we're all set."

"Ah? Because on top of everything else you spy on each other? You leave the dirty work to your unfortunate colleagues and then you go to town, huh? Shame on you. And maybe you think you're more intelligent because you ask brilliant ques-tions of the 'Are you in favor of war?' kind? And do you think I have been a universally admired writer of genius, who has received the Nobel Prize for literature, all so that a greenhorn can come and pester me with tautological questions, of the sort that even the dumbest of the dumb could answer with a reply identical to my own!"

"Fine. So, let's suppose you do not like war, but do you want the war to go ahead?"

"In the current state of affairs, it's a necessity. All those stupid little soldiers have a hard on. You have to give them the opportunity to ejaculate, otherwise they'll get pimples and they'll go home crying to their mommies. It's unkind to disappoint young people."

"Do you like young people, Monsieur Tach?"

"You have a gift for asking brilliant, unusual questions, I'll say that much. Yes, would you believe, I do like young people."

"That's rather unexpected. From what I know of you, I would have imagined you couldn't stand them."

"'From what I know of you'! Who do you think you are?"

"Well, knowing your reputation . . ."

"And what is my reputation?"

"Well . . . it's hard to say."

"Uh-huh. Out of consideration for you, I won't insist."

"So, you like young people? For what reason?"

"I like young people because they are everything I am not. And as such, they deserve tenderness and admiration."

"That is an astonishing reply, Monsieur Tach."

"Would you like a handkerchief?"

"Why are you making fun of your more noble sentiments?"

"My 'more noble sentiments'? Where the devil do you go to find such utter nonsense?"

"I am sorry, sir, you yourself inspired me: what you said about young people was truly moving."

"Dig a little deeper, and you will see if it's moving."

"Then let us dig a bit deeper."

"As I was saying, I like young people because they are everything I am not. Which is to say, young people are attractive, nimble, stupid, and nasty."

The journalist looked at him in questioning silence.

"Don't you agree? An astonishing reply, to use your own words."

"I suppose you are joking?"

"Do I look like someone who jokes? And what would be funny about this? Can you refute even one of those adjectives?"

"Even if we were to admit the adjectives are appropriate, do you really think you are at the opposite pole?"

"What? Or do you think I am attractive, nimble, stupid, and nasty?"

"You are neither attractive, nor nimble, nor stupid . . ."

"Well, that is reassuring at least."

"But as for nasty—well, that you are!"

"Nasty, me?"

"Absolutely."

"Nasty? You are sick. I have lived eighty-three years, and I have never met anyone as incredibly kind as my own self. I am a monster of kindness; I am so kind that if I met myself, I would vomit."

"You can't be serious."

"This is too much. Find me one individual, not better than I am (that would be impossible), but as kind as I am."

"Well . . . just anybody."

"Just anybody? You yourself then, if I've understood correctly? You must be joking."

"Me, or anybody."

"Don't talk about just anybody, you don't know them. Talk to me about yourself. What gives you the right to claim you are as kind as I am?"

"I have the most flagrant proof."

"Uh-huh. Just as I thought, you have no arguments."

"Really, Monsieur Tach, stop talking nonsense, would you? I listened to the two interviews with the previous journalists. Even if all I knew about you were based on those samples, I would already know what to expect from you. Can you deny that you tortured those two poor fellows?"

"Such bad faith! They are the ones who tortured me!"

"Just in case you were unaware of the fact, both of them have been sick as dogs since their dealings with you."

"*Post hoc, ergo propter hoc*, don't you think? You are drawing up a relation of cause and effect that is altogether eccentric, young man. The first journalist fell ill after drinking too many egg flips. You're not about to tell me that I'm the one who made him drink them, I hope? The second one badgered me, against my will, to make me talk about my eating habits. If he could not stomach my detailed descriptions, that's not my fault, now is it? I would like to add that both those individuals behaved most arrogantly toward me. Oh, I put up with it, I was as gentle as a lamb on the sacrificial altar. But they must have suffered. You see, it always comes back to the Gospels: Christ said as much, that those who are nasty and hateful harm themselves first and foremost. Whence the torment endured by your colleagues."

"Monsieur Tach, may I ask you to respond in all sincerity to the following question: do you take me for an imbecile?"

"Naturally."

"Thank you for your sincerity."

"Don't thank me, I am incapable of lying. Moreover, I cannot understand why you are asking me this question when you know the answer already: you are young, and I have not hidden from you what I think about young people."

"Speaking of which, don't you think you're lacking in nuance somewhat? You can't put all young people in the same bag."

"I'll grant you that. Some young people are neither attractive nor nimble. You, for example, I don't know if you're nimble, but you are anything but attractive."

"Thank you for that. And what about nastiness and stupidity, are there no exceptions where young people are concerned?"

"I've known only one exception: myself."

"What were you like, at the age of twenty?"

"Just as I am now. I could still walk. Otherwise, I don't see how I have changed. I was already hairless, obese, mystical, genial, ugly, too kind, supremely intelligent, and solitary, and I already liked to eat and smoke."

"In other words, you had no youth?"

"I love to listen to you talk, I could swear you're a feast of platitudes. I will agree to the statement, 'Yes, I had no youth,' on the following tacit condition: be sure to specify in your article that this was your expression. Otherwise, people might think that Prétextat Tach is in the habit of using terminology from airport novels."

"I'll be sure to do so. And now, if you have no objections, please explain to me why you think you are so good, with examples to back up your arguments, if possible."

"I love your 'if possible.' You don't believe in my goodness, then, do you?"

"Believe is not the appropriate verb here. Let's just say, rather, I have difficulty imagining it."

"Well, I never. Young man, try to imagine what my life has been: a sacrifice lasting eighty-three years. What was Christ's sacrifice, in comparison? My passion has lasted for fifty years or more. And before long I shall undergo an infinitely more remarkable apotheosis, that will be longer, more exclusive, and perhaps even more painful: a slow death that will leave on my flesh the glorious stigmata of the Elzenveiverplatz Syndrome. Our Lord inspires the most noble sentiments in me, but with all the good will in the world, I could not imagine Him dying of cartilage cancer."

"And so?"

"What do you mean, and so? Do you think it's the same thing, whether one dies from crucifixion, which was ordinary as rain back in those days, or from an extremely rare syndrome?"

"It's still death, one way or the other."

"My God! Have you any idea of the nonsense your tape recorder has just recorded? And your colleagues are going to hear this! My poor fellow, I would not like to be in your shoes.

'Still death, one way or the other.' I'm so kind that I will grant you permission to erase that."

"It's out of the question, Monsieur Tach, and that truly is my opinion."

"Do you know that I am beginning to find you fascinating? Such a lack of discernment is extraordinary. You should be transferred to the 'Run-over dogs' department, learn dog language and ask these poor dying animals if they would not have preferred to die from an exceptional disease."

"Monsieur Tach, do you ever speak to people other than to insult them?"

"I never insult people, Monsieur, I diagnose. In fact, I suppose you have never read any of my works?"

"You're mistaken."

"What? That's impossible. You have neither the demeanor nor the attitude of a typical Tachian reader. You must be lying."

"It's the absolute truth. I have read only one of your novels, but I read it thoroughly, then I reread it, and it had a lasting impact on me."

"You must be confusing it with something else."

"How could anyone confuse a book like *Gratuitous Rape Between Two Wars* with another? Believe me, I was deeply shaken by your work."

"Shaken? Shaken! As if I wrote to shake people! If you didn't merely skim the book, Monsieur, as I suspect you did, if you read it the way it was meant to be read, with your guts—provided you even have any—you would have thrown up."

"There is indeed an emetic esthetic in your oeuvre."

"An emetic esthetic! You are hell-bent on making me weep!"

"Anyway, to get back to what we were saying earlier, I can safely assert that I have never read anything more bloated with nastiness."

"Precisely. You wanted proof of my kindness: you have it,

and it is flagrant. Céline understood as much, and in his prefaces he said he wrote his most poisonous books out of disinterested kindness, out of an irrepressible tenderness for his detractors. That is true love."

"That's a bit much, no?"

"Céline, a bit much? You'd do better to erase that."

"No, really, that unbearably nasty scene with the deaf-mute woman, one can tell you were jubilant when you wrote it."

"To be sure. You cannot imagine the pleasure one derives from bringing grist to the mill of one's detractors."

"Ah! In that case, it isn't goodness, Monsieur Tach, but an obscure mixture of masochism and paranoia."

"Ta, ta, ta! Stop using words you don't even understand. Pure goodness, young man! Which books, in your opinion, have been written out of pure goodness? *Uncle Tom's Cabin*? *Les Misérables*? Of course not. Those books were written so that their authors would be made welcome in drawing rooms. No, believe me, books written out of pure kindness are rare indeed. Such works are created in abjection and solitude, with the terrible knowledge that once they are thrown out into the world, their author shall be even more alone and more abject. That's normal, the primary characteristic of disinterested goodness is to be unrecognizable, unknown, invisible, and above suspicion—because a good deed that says its name is never disinterested. As you can see, I am good."

"There's a paradox in what you've just said. You tell me that true goodness is hidden, and then you shout out loud that you are good."

"Oh, I can allow myself to do so as much as I like, because, in any event, no one will believe me."

The journalist burst out laughing.

"Your arguments are truly fascinating, Monsieur Tach. So you claim to have devoted your entire life to writing—out of pure goodness?"

"And there are many other things that I have been in the habit of doing out of pure goodness."

"For example?"

"The list is long: celibacy, gluttony, et cetera."

"Would you care to explain?"

"Of course, goodness has never been my only motive. Take celibacy: it is a well-known fact that I have no interest in sex. But I could have gotten married all the same, if only for the pleasure of making my spouse's life miserable. Well I didn't, because my goodness intervened: I forswore marriage in order to spare the unfortunate woman."

"So be it. And gluttony?"

"What could be more obvious: I am the Messiah of obesity. When I die, I will take all the excess pounds of humankind onto my shoulders."

"You mean that, symbolically . . ."

"Careful! Don't ever use the word 'symbol' in my presence, unless you're talking about chemistry: it's in your own interest."

"Forgive me if I'm being stupid and obtuse, but to be honest I don't understand."

"It's doesn't matter, you are not alone."

"Couldn't you explain it to me?"

"I despise wasting my time."

"Monsieur Tach, even supposing that I am stupid and obtuse, can't you imagine that behind me somewhere there is a future reader of this article, an intelligent, open reader who does deserve to understand? And who might be disappointed by what you've just said?"

"And supposing this reader exists: if he is truly intelligent and open, he won't need any explanation."

"I don't agree. Even an intelligent individual needs an explanation when he is confronted with a new and unknown idea."

"What do you know? You've never been intelligent."

"That's as may be, but I am humbly trying to imagine."

"My poor boy."

"Go on, show me your proverbial kindness and explain it to me."

"Do you really want to know? Truly intelligent, open people do not beg for explanations. Nothing is more vulgar than to have everything explained, including the things that are inexplicable. So why should I provide you with an explanation that an idiot would not understand and a more astute individual could not care less about?"

"Already I am ugly, stupid, and obtuse, and now I must add vulgar, is that it?"

"I cannot keep secrets from you."

"If I may be so bold, Monsieur Tach, this is not the way to go about trying to make people like you."

"Make people like me? That's all I need. Besides, who are you to come and preach to me, less than two months before my glorious death? Who do you think you are? You began your sentence with 'If I may be so bold,' well, you may not be so bold! Go on, get out, you're bothering me."

The journalist was dumbfounded.

"Are you deaf?"

Sheepish, the journalist joined his colleagues in the café across the street. He did not know whether he had gotten off lightly or not.

As they listened to the tape, his colleagues didn't say anything, but it was most certainly not at Tach that they aimed their condescending smiles.

"That man is really a case," said the most recent victim. "Go figure! You never know how he's going to react. Sometimes you get the impression he'll listen to anything, that nothing fazes him, that he even enjoys it if you nuance your questions with some impertinent remarks. And then suddenly without warning he goes and explodes because of a ridiculous detail, or he throws you out the door if you have the unfortunate wisdom to make a tiny, legitimate remark."

"Genius cannot bear any commentary," said one of his colleagues, as haughtily as if he were Tach himself.

"What, then? Should I have let myself be insulted?"

"The ideal thing would have been not to give him cause for any insults."

"Very clever! For him, that's all the world does, give cause for insults!"

"Poor Tach! Poor exiled titan."

"Poor Tach? That's the limit. Poor us, you mean!"

"Don't you understand that we are bothering him?"

"Yes, I did realize that. But someone has to do our job, no?"

"Why?" said the other man, feeling inspired, after spitting in the soup.

"Then why did you become a journalist, jerk?"

"Because I couldn't be Prétextat Tach."

"You would have enjoyed being a huge graphomaniac eunuch?"

Yes, he would have enjoyed it, and he was not the only one to contemplate the idea. The human race is made in such a way that many a person of sound mind would be prepared to sacrifice youth, beauty, health, love, friendship, happiness, and much, much more on the altar of an illusion known as eternity.

W ell, has the war begun?"

"Uh . . . yes, it has, the first missiles have—"

"Excellent."

"Really?"

"I don't like to see young people sitting around with nothing to do. So at last, on this day of January 17, those young kids are having a good time."

"In a manner of speaking."

"What, don't you think it would be fun?"

"Frankly, no."

"Maybe you think it is more fun to go running after a fat old man with a tape recorder?"

"Run after? But we're not running after you, you yourself gave us permission to come."

"Never! It was another trick of Gravelin's, that old dog."

"Go on, Monsieur Tach, you are perfectly free to say no to your secretary, he's a devoted man who respects your every wish."

"You don't know what you're talking about. He torments me and never consults me. The nurse, for example, that's all his doing."

"Come now, Monsieur Tach, calm down. Let's go on with the interview. How do you explain the extraordinary success—"

"Would you like a Brandy Alexander?"

"No, thank you. As I was saying, the extraordinary success of—"

"Wait, I would like one."

Alchemical interlude.

"This brand-new war has given me a raging thirst for Brandy Alexanders. It is such a solemn beverage."

"Right. Monsieur Tach, How do you explain the extraordinary success of your novels the world over?"

"I don't explain it."

"Go on, you must have thought about it and come up with some answers."

"No."

"No? You have sold millions of copies, even in China, and this doesn't make you think?"

"Weapons factories sell thousands of missiles the world over every day, and that doesn't make them think, either."

"There's no comparison."

"You don't think so? And yet there is a striking parallel. There's an accumulation, for example: we talk about an arms race, we should also talk about a 'literature race.' It's a cogent argument like any other: every nation brandishes its writer or writers as if they were cannons. Sooner or later I too will be brandished, and they'll prepare my Nobel Prize for battle."

"If that's the way you look at it, I have to agree with you. But thank God, literature is less harmful."

"Not mine. My literature is even more harmful than war."

"Don't you think you're flattering yourself there?"

"Well, I'm obliged to, because I am the only reader who is capable of understanding me. Yes, my books are more harmful than war, because they make you want to die, whereas war, in fact, makes you want to live. After reading me, people should feel like committing suicide."

"And how do you explain the fact that they don't?"

"Well, I can explain it very easily: it is because nobody reads me. Basically, that may also be the reason for my extraordinary success: if I am so famous, my good man, it is because nobody reads me."

"But that's a paradox!"

"On the contrary: if these poor folk had tried to read me, they would have disliked me from the start and, to avenge themselves for the effort they wasted on me, they would have consigned me to oblivion. But because they do not read me, they find me restful and therefore I am to their liking and deserving of success."

"That is an extraordinary argument."

"But it is irrefutable. Take Homer, for example: now there is a writer who has never been this famous. Yet do you know many people who have truly read the real Iliad, or the real Odyssey? A handful of bald philologists, that's all—because you can't really qualify as readers a few dozy high school students mumbling their way through Homer in the classroom when all they're thinking about is Depeche Mode or AIDS. And it is precisely for that excellent reason that Homer is *the* authority."

"But assuming this is true, do you really think it's an excellent argument? Is it not regrettable, rather?"

"I insist that it is excellent. Is it not comforting for a true, pure, great genius of a writer like myself to know that no one reads me? That no trivial gaze has sullied the beauty to which I have given birth in the secrecy of my inner self and of my solitude?"

"To avoid that trivial gaze, would it not have been simpler not to get published at all?"

"That would be too easy. No, you see, the *nec plus ultra* of refinement is to sell millions of copies and never be read."

"Not to mention the fact that you have earned a great deal of money."

"Certainly. I do like money."

"You like money, do you?"

"Yes. It's ravishing. I've never found it useful, but I do enjoy looking at it. A five franc coin is as pretty as a daisy."

"Now, such a comparison would have never occurred to me."

"That's normal, you are not a Nobel laureate."

"Basically, doesn't your Nobel Prize go against your theory? Doesn't it oblige us to assume that at least the Nobel committee has read your work?"

"I wouldn't bank on it. But in the event that the committee members did read me, you can be sure that it wouldn't change anything about my theory. There are a great many people who push sophistication to the point of reading without reading. They're like frogmen, they go through books without absorbing a single drop of water."

"Yes, you mentioned them in a previous interview."

"Those are the frog-readers. They make up the vast majority of human readers, and yet I only discovered their existence quite late in life. I am so terribly naïve. I thought that everyone read the way I do. For I read the way I eat: that means not only do I need to read, but also, and above all, that reading becomes one of my components and modifies them all. You are not the same person depending on whether you have eaten blood pudding or caviar; nor are you the same person depending on whether you have just read Kant (God help us) or Queneau. Well, when I say 'you,' I should say 'I myself and a few others,' because the majority of people emerge from reading Proust or Simenon in an identical state: they have neither lost a fraction of what they were nor gained a single additional fraction. They have read, that's all: in the best-case scenario, they know 'what it's about.' And I'm not exaggerating. How often have I asked intelligent people, 'Did this book change you?' And they look at me, their eyes wide, as if to say, 'Why should a book to change me?'"

"Allow me to express my astonishment, Monsieur Tach: you have just spoken as if you were defending books with a message, and that's not like you."

"You're not very clever, are you? So are you of the opinion that only books 'with a message' can change an individual?

Those are the books that are the least likely to change them. The books that have an impact, that transform people, are the other ones—books about desire, or pleasure, books filled with genius, and above all books filled with beauty. Let us take, for example, a great book filled with beauty: *Journey to the End of the Night.* How can you not be transformed after you have read it? Well, the majority of readers manage just that tour de force without difficulty. They will come to you and say, 'Oh yes, Céline is magnificent,' and then they go back to what they were doing. Obviously, Céline is an extreme example, but I could mention others, too. You are never the same after you have read a book, even as modest a work as one by Léo Malet: one of his books will change you. You will never again look at young women in raincoats in the same way once you've read a book by Léo Malet. Really, this is extremely important! Changing the way people see things: that is our magnum opus."

"Don't you think that, consciously or unconsciously, everybody changes the way they see things after they have finished a book?"

"Oh, no! Only the crème de la crème of readers can do that. The others go on seeing things with their usual flatness. And here we are only talking about readers, who in themselves are a very rare species. Most people do not read. In this regard, there is an excellent quotation by an intellectual whose name I have forgotten: 'Basically, people do not read; or, if they do read, they don't understand; or, if they do understand, they forget.' An admirable summing-up of the situation, don't you agree?"

"If that is the case, is it not tragic to be a writer?"

"If there is something tragic about the situation, that is certainly not the reason. It is beneficial not to be read. You can write whatever you like."

"But in the beginning, someone must have read you, otherwise you would not have become famous."

"In the beginning, perhaps, a little bit."

"Which brings me back to my initial question: how do you explain your extraordinary success? Why did your early novels touch a nerve with readers?"

"I don't know. That was back in the 1930s. There was no television, people had to find something to keep busy."

"Yes, but why you, rather than another writer?"

"The truth is, it was after the war that I began to be so successful. Which is amusing when you think about it, because I was in no way involved with that huge farce: I was already virtually a total invalid, and ten years earlier, I had been declared unfit for service because of my obesity. In 1945 the great expiation began: whether they were confused or not, people felt they had reasons to be ashamed. So when they happened upon my novels, which seemed to be screaming with imprecations and were overflowing with filth, they decided they had found a punishment commensurate with their own baseness."

"And was it?"

"It might have been. But it might have been something else, too. But there you are, *vox populi, vox dei*. And then very quickly they stopped reading me. As with Céline, moreover: Céline is probably one of the least read of all writers. The difference is that I wasn't being read for the right reasons, whereas he wasn't being read for the wrong reasons."

"You often refer to Céline."

"I love literature, sir. Are you surprised?"

"You do not expurgate him, I gather?"

"No. He's the one who is constantly expurgating me."

"Have you met him?"

"No, I've done better than that: I've read him."

"And has he read you?"

"Certainly. I could often sense as much when I was reading him."

"You think you have influenced Céline?"

"Less than he influenced me, but still."

"And who else might you have influenced?"

"No one, obviously, because no one else has read me. Although, thanks to Céline, I have been read—truly read—at least once."

"So you see that you do want to be read."

"By him, only by him. I don't give a damn about other people."

"Have you met other writers?"

"No, I have met no one and no one has come to meet me. I know very few people: Gravelin, of course, and apart from him, the butcher, the milkman, the grocer, and the tobacconist. That's all, I think. Oh yes, there's also that bitch of a nurse, and the journalists. I don't like to see people. If I live alone, it's not so much because I love solitude but that I hate humankind. You can write in your rag that I'm a filthy misanthropist."

"Why are you a misanthropist?"

"You haven't read *Filthy People*, I suppose?"

"No."

"Naturally. If you had read it, you would know why. There are a thousand reasons to despise people. The most important one, for me, is their bad faith, which is incorrigible. What's more, nowadays, this bad faith is more widespread than ever. You can well imagine that I have lived through a number of eras: nevertheless, I can assure you that never have I so despised an era the way I do this one. An era of full-blown bad faith. Bad faith is worse than disloyalty, duplicity, perfidy. If you are in bad faith, first of all you are lying to yourself, not because you are struggling with your conscience, but for your own syrupy self-satisfaction, using pretty names like 'modesty' or 'dignity.' And then you're lying to other people, but not with honest, nasty lies, not to stir up shit, no: your lies are those of a hypocrite, a *lite* liar, ranting and raving with a smile, as if this would make everyone happy."

"For example?"

"Well, the condition of women in this day and age."

"In what way? Are you a feminist?"

"Me, a feminist? I hate women even more than I hate men."

"Why?"

"For a thousand reasons. First of all, because they are ugly: have you ever seen anything uglier than a woman? What a senseless idea to have breasts, and hips—I'll spare you the rest. And then, I hate women the way I hate all victims. A filthy race, victims. If we were to exterminate them altogether, perhaps we'd have peace at last, and perhaps at last the victims would get what they want, which is martyrdom. Women are particularly pernicious victims because they are, above all else, the victims of other women. If you want to penetrate the dregs of human emotions, take a good look at the feelings that women cultivate toward other women: you will tremble with horror at the sight of so much hypocrisy, jealousy, nastiness, and iniquity. You will never see two women having a good healthy fistfight or even flinging a good volley of insults at each other: with women, it's the nasty tricks that triumph, the vile little phrases that hurt far more than a good punch in the jaw. You'll tell me there's nothing new about all that, that the world of women has been like this since Adam and Eve. But I will tell you that the lot of women has never been worse, and it's their own fault, we agree on that, but what does that change? The condition of women has become the arena for truly disgusting manifestations of bad faith."

"You still haven't explained anything."

"Let's look at the way things used to be. Women are inferior to men, that goes without saying: all you have to do is see how ugly they are. In the past, there was no bad faith. No one tried to hide women's inferiority, and they were treated in consequence. But what we have nowadays is revolting: women are still inferior to men—for they are still just as ugly—but they are being told that they are man's equal. And because they are stupid, naturally they believe it. Yet women are still being treated as inferior: salaries are merely one minor sign of this. There are others that are far more serious: women are still far behind in every domain—charm, to begin with—there's nothing surprising about that, given how ugly they are, and how little intelligence they have, and given above all their disgusting spitefulness, which crops up at the first opportunity. You have to admire the bad faith of the system: take an ugly, stupid, nasty, charmless slave and make her believe that she is starting off with the same opportunities as her master—when in fact she has only a quarter as many. Personally I find it appalling. If I were a woman, I would be sick."

"But you do conceive, I hope, that other people might not agree with you?"

"'Conceive' is not the appropriate verb. I do not conceive it, I am offended by it. What perfidy will you invoke to contradict me?"

"My own taste, to begin with. I don't think women are ugly."

"My poor friend, you have potty taste."

"A woman's breasts are a beautiful thing."

"You don't know what you're saying. Already on the glossy paper of a magazine those female protuberances are at the limit of what is acceptable. What about the ones belonging to real women, the ones they dare not show and which make up the vast majority of tits? Yuck."

"That's just your taste. We're not obliged to share it."

"Oh, of course, you might even think a lump of fat sold at the butcher's is a thing of beauty: nothing is forbidden."

"That has nothing to do with it."

"Women are filthy slabs of meat. Sometimes it is said of a particularly ugly woman that she is a lump of fat: the truth of the matter is that all women are lumps of fat."

"Allow me to ask you then what you think you are!"

"A lump of lard. Can you not tell?"

"So do you think that men are beautiful?"

"I didn't say that. Men's bodies are less horrible than women's. But that does not make them beautiful."

"So no one is beautiful?"

"No, some children are very beautiful. Unfortunately, it does not last."

"Do you consider childhood to be a blessed time?"

"Did you hear what you've just said? 'Childhood is a blessed time.'"

"It's a cliché, but it's true, no?"

"Of course it's true, animal! But is it necessary to say so? Everybody knows it."

"Monsieur Tach, you are a wretched person."

"And you only just figured that out? You need some rest, young man, so much genius is going to wear you out."

"What is the source of your despair?"

"Everything. It's not just the world that is badly made, but life. Another feature of contemporary bad faith is the way we go around claiming the opposite. Haven't you ever heard them all bleating unanimously, 'Life is beaueau-ti-ful! We love life!' It makes me climb the walls to hear such drivel."

"Such drivel may be sincere."

"I believe that too, which makes it even worse: it proves that treachery is working, that people will swallow any lie. So they have their shitty lives with their shitty jobs, they live in horrible places with dreadful people, and they embrace their abject condition and then call it happiness."

"Good for them, if they're happy that way!"

"Good for them, as you say."

"And you, Monsieur Tach, what makes you happy?"

"Nothing at all. I have peace and quiet, that's already something—well, I did have peace and quiet."

"Have you never been happy?"

Silence.

"Am I to understand that you have been happy? . . . Or am I to understand that you have never been happy?"

"Be quiet, I'm thinking. No, I have never been happy."

"That's terrible."

"Would you like a handkerchief?"

"Even during your childhood?"

"I was never a child."

"What do you mean by that?"

"Exactly what I said."

"Well you must have been little!"

"I was little, yes, but I was not a child. I was already Prétextat Tach."

"It's true that we know nothing about your childhood. Your biographers always start with your adult life."

"That's normal, because I had no childhood."

"But you had parents, after all."

"You do pile on your brilliant conclusions, young man."

"What did your parents do?"

"Nothing."

"What do you mean?"

"They lived off their income. A very old family fortune."

"Are there any other family members besides yourself?"

"Was it the tax man who sent you?"

"No, I just wanted to know if—"

"Mind your own business."

"One's duty as a journalist, Monsieur Tach, is to mind other people's business."

"Change your profession."

"That's out of the question. I like my profession."

"My poor boy."

"Let me put it to you in another way: tell me about the time in your life when you were happiest."

Silence.

"Should I phrase my question in another way?"

"Do you take me for a fool or what? What sort of game are you playing at? Is this some sort of *Belle marquise, vos beaux yeux me font mourir d'amour*? Is that it?"

"Calm down, I'm just trying to do my job."

"And I'm trying to do mine."

"So in your opinion, a writer is someone whose job consists in not answering questions?"

"Exactly."

"And Sartre?"

"What about Sartre?"

"Well, he answered questions, didn't he?"

"So what?"

"That contradicts your definition."

"Not in the least: it confirms it, on the contrary."

"You mean that Sartre is not a writer?"

"You didn't know?"

"What do you mean, he wrote remarkably well."

"There are journalists who write remarkably well. But it is not enough to have a way with words to be a writer."

"No? What else is required, then?"

"A great many things. First of all, you need balls. And the balls I am referring to have nothing to do with one's sex. The proof of it is that there are some women who have balls. Oh, not very many, but they do exist: Patricia Highsmith, for example."

"That's astonishing, that a great writer like yourself would like the work of Patricia Highsmith."

"Why? There's nothing astonishing about it at all. You might not think so, but she's someone who must hate people as much as I do, and women in particular. You can tell she doesn't write in order to be invited to people's drawing rooms."

"And what about Sartre, did he write in order to be invited to drawing rooms?"

"Did he ever! I never met the gentleman, but just reading him I could tell how much he loved drawing rooms."

"That's a bit hard to swallow. He was a leftist, after all."

"So? Do you think leftists don't like drawing rooms? I think that, on the contrary, they like them more than anyone. It stands to reason: if I'd been a worker all my life, it seems to me I would like nothing better than to spend my time in drawing rooms."

"You're oversimplifying: not all leftists are workers. Some leftists come from very good families."

"Really? Then they have no excuse."

"You wouldn't happen to be a rabid anti-Communist, would you, Monsieur Tach?"

"And you wouldn't you happen to be a premature ejaculator, now would you, Mr. Journalist?"

"Oh, really, that has nothing to do with it."

"I do agree. So, to get back to our balls. They are the most vital organ a writer has. If he has no balls, a writer uses his words in the service of bad faith. To give you an example, let's take a gifted writer, and give him something to write about. With solid balls, you get *Death on Credit*. Without balls, you get *La nausée*."

"Don't you think you're simplifying somewhat?"

"Are you, a journalist, serious? And here I've been trying, out of the goodness of my heart, to bring myself down to your level!"

"I never asked you to. What I want is a precise and methodical definition of what you mean by 'balls.'"

"Why? Don't tell me you are trying to write some sort of Tach Made Easy for the general public?"

"Not at all! I just wanted to have some sort of clear communication with you."

"Uh-huh, that's what I was afraid of."

"Come now, Monsieur Tach, please try and make things simple for me, just for once."

"You must understand that I detest any form of simplification, young man; so if you start asking me to simplify myself, don't expect me to be very enthusiastic."

"But I'm not asking you to simplify yourself, not at all! I'm just asking you for a brief definition of what you mean by 'balls.'"

"All right, all right, don't whine. What is it with you journalists? You are all so hypersensitive."

"I'm listening."

"Well, balls are an individual's ability to resist the prevailing bad faith. Sounds scientific, right?"

"Go on."

"I might as well tell you that almost no one has the balls for it. And the number of people who have both a way with words and the right kind of balls is infinitesimal. That is why there are so few writers on the planet. Particularly as other qualities are also required."

"Such as?"

"A prick."

"After balls, a prick: that's logical. Definition of prick?"

"The prick is an ability to create. People who are truly capable of creating are rare indeed. Most of them are content with merely copying their predecessors with greater or lesser degrees of talent—and those same predecessors are, most often, copiers themselves. Sometimes you get a writer who has a way with words and a prick but no balls: Victor Hugo, for example."

"And yourself?"

"I may have the face of a eunuch, but I have a big prick."

"And Céline?"

"Ah, Céline has everything: he's a genius with words, and he has big balls, a big prick, and all the rest."

"The rest? What else is required? An anus?"

"Absolutely not! It's the reader who must have an anus, to be taken for a fool, not the writer. No, a writer also needs lips."

"Dare I even ask you what kind of lips you mean?"

"Upon my word, you are revolting! I'm talking about the lips that are used to close one's mouth, all right? Disgusting individual!"

"Okay. Definition of lips?"

"Lips fulfill two roles. First of all, they make words into a sensual act. Have you ever imagined what words would be were it not for lips? They would quite simply be something cold, dry, without any nuances, like the utterances of a courtroom bailiff. But the second role is even more important: lips are used to prevent what must not be said from getting out. Hands also have lips, the lips that prevent them from writing what must not be written. This is indispensable, beyond all proportion. There are writers who are brimming with talent, who have balls and a prick, yet they failed as writers because they said things they shouldn't have said."

"That's astonishing, coming from you: it's not your style to practice self-censorship."

"Who said anything about self-censorship? The things that must not be said are not necessarily smutty things; on the contrary. The smutty things you have inside you must always be expressed: that's healthy, lighthearted, invigorating. No, the things that must not be said are of another order—and don't expect me to explain them to you, because those are precisely the things that must not be said."

"Well that's not going to get me very far."

"Didn't I warn you, earlier, that my profession consists in not answering questions? Change your profession, young man."

"So not answering questions is also one of the roles fulfilled by lips, is that it?"

"Not only lips, balls too. It takes balls not to answer certain questions."

"A way with words, balls, a prick, lips—anything else?"

"Yes, you also need an ear and a hand."

"The ear is for hearing?"

"You heard me. You are a regular genius, young man. In fact, the ear is the sound box of the lips. It's the inner *gueuloir*.

Flaubert struck quite the pose with his *gueuloir*, but did he really think people were going to believe him? He knew it was pointless to holler his words: words holler all by themselves. You just have to listen to them inside."

"And the hand?"

"The hand is for pleasure. This is devastatingly important. If a writer is not having pleasure, then he must stop immediately. To write without pleasure is immoral. Writing already contains all the seeds of immorality. The writer's only excuse is his pleasure. A writer who does not have pleasure is as disgusting as some bastard raping a little girl without even getting his rocks off, just for the sake of raping, to commit a gratuitously evil act."

"There's no comparison. Writing is not as harmful."

"You obviously don't know what you're saying, because you haven't read me—how could you know? Writing fucks things up at every level: think of the trees they've had to cut down for the paper, of all the room they have to find to store the books, the money it costs to print them, and the money it will cost potential readers, and the boredom the readers will feel on reading them, and the guilty conscience of the unfortunate people who buy them and don't have the courage to read them, and the sadness of the kind imbeciles who do read them but don't understand a thing, and finally, above all, the fatuousness of the conversations that will take place after said books have been read or not read. And that's just the half of it! So don't go telling me that writing is not harmful."

"But you can't totally rule out the possibility of encountering one or two readers who really will understand you, even if it's only intermittently. Don't those flashes of deep complicity with a handful of individuals suffice to make reading a beneficial act?"

"Nonsense! I don't know if those individuals exist, but, if they do, they are the ones who can be most harmed by what I write. What do you think I talk about in my books? Maybe you think I describe how good human beings are, how happy they are to be alive? How the devil did you come up with the idea that to understand me will make someone happy? On the contrary!"

"But complicity, even in despair—is that not a pleasant thing?"

"Do you think it's pleasant to find out that you are just as desperate as your neighbor? I think it makes things even sadder."

"In that case, why write? Why even seek to communicate?"

"Careful, don't mix up the two: writing is not seeking to communicate. You ask me why I write, and this is what I'd say, strictly and exclusively: for pleasure. In other words, if there is no pleasure, one must stop, imperatively. It so happens that writing brings me pleasure—well, it used to—so much pleasure I could die. Don't ask me why, I have no idea. Moreover, every theory that has tried to explain pleasure has been more inane than the next one. One day, a very serious man told me that when you felt pleasure in making love, it was because you were creating life. Can you imagine? As if there could be pleasure in creating something as bad and ugly as life! And then, that would imply that if a woman is taking the pill, she should no longer feel pleasure because she's no longer creating life. But this fellow really believed his theory! In short, don't ask me to explain why writing gives me pleasure: it's a fact, that's all."

"And what has the hand got to do with all this?"

"The hand is the source of pleasure in writing. And it's not the only one: writing also brings pleasure to one's belly, one's sex, one's forehead, and one's jaws. But the most specific pleasure is located in the hand that writes. It's a difficult thing to explain: when it is creating what it needs to create, the hand trembles with pleasure and becomes an organ of genius. I don't know how many times while writing I have had the strange impression that my hand was in charge, sliding across the page all alone, without asking the brain its opinion. Oh, I know that no anatomist could accept such a thing, and yet very often that is what you feel. It is such a voluptuous moment, probably not unlike what a horse feels when it bolts, or a prisoner when he escapes. Which leads to another conclusion: is there not something disturbing about the fact that one uses the same instrument—one's hand—for both writing and masturbation?"

"You also use your hand to sew on a button or scratch your nose."

"How trivial you can be! Besides, what does that prove? The vulgar uses need not contradict the noble ones!"

"So masturbation is a noble use of the hand?"

"Indeed it is! The fact that, all alone, a simple, modest hand can perform something as complex, costly, tricky, and volatile as sex, isn't that amazing? To think that this kindly, uncomplicated hand can procure as much, if not more, pleasure than a woman—who is a high-maintenance nuisance—isn't that admirable?"

"Well, naturally, if that's the way you see things . . ."

"But that's the way they are, young man! Don't you agree?"

"Listen, Monsieur Tach, you are the one being interviewed, not me."

"In other words, you get off easy, is that it?"

"It may please you to know that I don't feel I've gotten off easy thus far. Here and there, you've been pretty rough with me."

"Something I enjoy doing, it's true."

"Fine. Let's get back to our organs. Let me recapitulate: a way with words, balls, prick, lips, ear, and hand. Is that it?"

"Isn't that enough for you?"

"I don't know. I thought there would be more."

"Really? What more do you need? A vulva? A prostate?"

"Now you're being trivial. No. Perhaps you're going to make fun of me, but I was thinking that you also need a heart."

"A heart? Saints alive, whatever for?"

"For feelings, love."

"Those things have nothing to do with the heart. They are the realm of the balls, prick, lips, and hands. That's quite enough."

"You're too cynical. I could never go along with that."

"But your opinion doesn't interest anyone, you said so yourself a minute ago. I don't see what is so cynical about what I said. Feelings and love are the business of organs, we agree on that; what we disagree on is only the nature of the organ. You see it as a cardiac phenomenon. I'm not rebelling against that idea, I'm not throwing adjectives in your face. I merely think that you have bizarre anatomical theories and, as such, they are interesting."

"Monsieur Tach, why are you pretending you don't understand?"

"Now what are you on about? I'm not pretending anything at all, you rude so-and-so!"

"Honestly, when I was talking about the heart, you know perfectly well I wasn't referring to the organ!"

"Oh, no? What were you referring to, then?"

"To sensitivity, affectivity, emotions, don't you see?"

"All that in one stupid heart, full of cholesterol!"

"Come now, Monsieur Tach, you're not being funny."

"No, indeed, you're the one who's being funny. Why are you saying all these things that have nothing to do with the topic of discussion?"

"Are you daring to imply that literature has nothing to do with feelings?"

"You know what, young man, I think our understandings of the word 'feeling' diverge. For me, if I want to smash someone's face in, that's a feeling. But for you, if you can weep at the lonely hearts column in a woman's magazine, now that's a feeling."

"And what is it for you?"

"For me, it is a frame of mind, that is, a fine story crammed full of deceitful ideas of which people convince themselves in order to procure an illusion of human dignity, and to persuade themselves that they are filled with spirituality even when they are taking a crap. It is above all women who invent such moods, because the type of work they do leaves their mind free. For one of the characteristics of our species is that our brain feels obliged to work continuously, even when it serves no purpose: this deplorable technical disadvantage is at the origin of all human misery. Rather than allowing her to indulge in noble inactivity or elegant repose, like a snake sleeping in the sun, the housewife's brain, furious that it is not being useful, begins to secrete idiotic, pretentious screenplays—and the baser the housewife perceives her activities to be, the more pretentious her scenarios become. And all the more stupid in that there is nothing base about running the vacuum cleaner or scrubbing the toilet: these are things that need to be done, that's all. But women always imagine that they have been placed here on earth for some aristocratic mission. Most men do, too, less stubbornly however, because their brains are kept busy with the help of bookkeeping, professional promotion, informing on their peers, and tax returns, which leave less time for wild imaginings."

"I think you're a bit behind the times. Women work now, too, and they have the same worries as men do."

"How naïve can you get! They're pretending. Their desk drawers are full of nail polish and women's magazines. Contemporary women are even worse than the housewives of old, who served some purpose at least. Nowadays, they spend their time chatting with their colleagues about subjects as substantial as relationships and calories, which amounts to the same thing. When they get too bored, they get laid by their bosses, which gives them a deliciously intoxicated feeling, knowing they are messing with other people's lives. What better professional promotion for a woman! When a woman destroys another person's life, she views her exploit as the supreme proof of her spirituality. 'I cause trouble, therefore I have a soul,' is how she reasons."

"To listen to you, anyone would think you have a score to settle with women."

"Indeed I do! One of them brought me into this world, although I certainly never asked her to."

"You sound just like a rebellious teenager."

"A bilious one would be more like it."

"Very funny. But a man had something to do with your birth, too."

"I don't like men, either, you know."

"But you do despise women more than men. Why?"

"For all the reasons I already gave you."

"Yes. But you see, I have difficulty believing you don't have another motive. Your misogyny stinks of a desire for revenge."

"Revenge? Whatever for? I've always been a bachelor."

"It's not just about marriage. Besides, maybe you yourself don't even know where your desire for revenge comes from."

"I can see where you're headed, and I refuse to be psycho-analyzed."

"Without going that far, you might spend some time thinking about it."

"Thinking about what, for God's sake?"

"Your relationships with women."

"What relationships? What women?"

"Don't tell me that you . . . No!"

"What, 'no'?"

"You're not a . . . ?"

"What, out with it!"

" . . . virgin?"

"Of course I am."

"Impossible."

"Absolutely possible."

"Neither with a woman, nor a man?"

"You think I look like a fag?"

"Don't take it badly, there have been some brilliant homosexuals."

"You make me laugh. You say that the way you would say, 'There have even been some honest pimps,' as if there were some contradiction between the words 'homosexual' and 'brilliant.' Still, I must protest against your refusal to accept that I might be a virgin."

"Put yourself in my shoes."

"How do you expect someone like me to put myself in your shoes?"

"But it's . . . it's unthinkable! In your novels, you talk about sex like a specialist, like an entomologist!"

"I have a Ph.D. in masturbation."

"Can masturbation result in such a thorough acquaintance with the flesh?"

"Why do you pretend that you've read me?"

"Look, I don't need to have read you to know that your name has been associated with a very precise, expert depiction of sex."

"How amusing. I didn't know that."

"I even came across a dissertation with the following title: 'Tachian Priapism as Expressed through Syntax.'"

"How droll. I've always had a soft spot for dissertation topics, I find them very entertaining. Those sweet students who, to imitate a great man, write idiotic things with hyper-sophisticated titles, when the contents are the very height of banality—like a pretentious restaurant embellishing scrambled eggs with a grandiose description."

"Naturally, Monsieur Tach, if you'd rather I wouldn't, I won't talk about your virginity."

"Why? Isn't it interesting?"

"On the contrary, it's extremely interesting. But I would not like to betray such a secret."

"It's not a secret."

"Why have you never spoken about it, then?"

"Who would I have spoken about it with? I don't go off to the butcher's to talk about my virginity."

"Of course not, but you shouldn't go telling the newspapers, either."

"Why not? Is virginity against the law?"

"It's just that it belongs to the sphere of your private life, your intimate world."

"And everything you've asked me up to now, you two-faced bastard, that didn't belong to my private life? You weren't so scrupulous a few minutes ago. It's pointless trying to play the blushing virgin (a case in point) with me all of a sudden, it won't wash."

"I don't agree. Where indiscretion is concerned, there are certain boundaries. A journalist is indiscreet by nature—it goes with the terrain—but he knows the limits."

"You're talking about yourself in the third person singular now?"

"I'm speaking in the name of all journalists."

"That's a typical reflex with your cowardly lot. I speak only in my own name, with no other guarantor than my own self. And I insist that I will not comply with your criteria: it's up to me to determine whether something, in my private life, is secret or not. I couldn't give a damn about my virginity: do whatever you like with it."

"Monsieur Tach, I believe you do not realize the danger of such a revelation: you ought to feel sullied, violated . . ."

"It's my turn to ask you a question, young man: are you stupid or merely masochistic?"

"Why do you ask?"

"Because if you're neither stupid nor masochistic, I can see no explanation for your behavior. Here I am giving you a superb scoop, making a noble gesture of disinterested generosity—but, instead of seizing the opportunity like an intelligent vulture, you start inventing scruples and making a fuss. And do you know what you are in danger of, if you go on like this? You are in danger that out of exasperation I might take your scoop away from you, not to preserve my sacrosanct private life, but quite simply to piss you off. I'll have you know that my spurts of generosity never last very long, above all when I get annoyed, so take heed at once and accept what I am offering you before I take it away. And you could thank me all the same, it's not every day that a Nobel Prize winner offers you his virginity, now is it?"

"You have my heartfelt thanks, Monsieur Tach."

"That's better. I love brown noses like you, dear boy."

"But you yourself asked me to—"

"And so what? You're not obliged to do everything I ask."

"All right. Let's go back to the previous subject. In the light of your most recent revelation, I believe I can understand the origins of your misogyny."

"Oh?"

"Yes, couldn't it be that your desire for revenge on women is founded in your virginity?"

"I fail to see the connection."

"But there is one: you despise women because none of them wanted anything to do with you."

The novelist burst out laughing. His shoulders were shaking.

"That's a good one! You're very funny, old boy."

"Am I to understand that you are refuting my explanation?"

"I think your explanation is self-refuting, my good man. You have just invented an edifying example of retrocausality—something journalists excel at, moreover. But you've done such a good job at reversing the issues that it's mind-boggling. So, you are inferring that I despise women because no woman has ever wanted anything to do with me, whereas in fact I wanted nothing to do with any of them, for the very simple reason that I despise them. A double reversal: well done, you are talented."

"You would have me believe that you despise women out of hand, for no good reason? That's impossible."

"Give me the name of a food that you despise."

"I hate skate, but—"

"Why such a desire for revenge on that poor skate?"

"I have no desire for revenge on skate; I've always found it inedible, and that's all."

"Well then, we understand each other. I have no desire for revenge on women, but I've always hated them, and that's all."

"But really, Monsieur Tach, there's no comparison. What would you say if I compared you to calf tongue?"

"I would be very flattered, calf tongue is delicious."

"Go on, be serious."

"I'm always serious. And more's the pity for you, young man, because if I were not so serious, perhaps I would not have noticed that this interview has gone on for an unprecedented length of time: you do not deserve such generosity on my part."

"What have I done not to deserve it?"

"You are ungrateful, and you are in bad faith."

"I'm in bad faith, me? And what about you?"

"You're insolent! I've always known that my good faith would never get me anywhere. Not only does no one notice it, but it is reversed—it's true that you are an expert in reversing things—and is qualified as bad faith. My sacrifice will have been in vain. At times I think that if I were to start over, I would play the bad faith card for all it's worth, so I could enjoy some of your peace of mind and respect. But then I look at you and find you so repugnant that I congratulate myself on not having imitated you, even if it has condemned me to solitude. Solitude can only do me good if it keeps me well away from your mire. My life may be nasty, but I prefer it to yours. Leave my home, Monsieur, I have just finished my tirade, so prove to me that you know how to take your cue, be so good as to leave my home."

In the café across the street, the journalist's story added fuel to the debate.

"Under these conditions, are we deontologically justified in continuing our interviews?"

"Tach would surely reply that we must be two-faced bastards to dare talk about deontology in our profession."

"That is certainly what he would say, but he isn't the pope, after all. We're under no obligation to put up with his dreadful nonsense."

"The problem is that his dreadful nonsense stinks of truth."

"Here we go, he's got you jumping through hoops. I'm sorry, but I have no respect for the guy anymore. He's too full of himself."

"It's just as he said: you're ungrateful. He gives you the dream of a story and to the only way you can think of to thank him is by heaping scorn on him."

"But didn't you hear how he insulted me?"

"Precisely. That's why you're so full of rage."

"I can't wait until it's your turn. Then we'll have a good laugh."

"I can't wait until it's my turn, either."

"And did you hear what he said about women?"

"Oh, he's not completely wrong on that score."

"Shame on you. It's a good job there are no women around to hear you. Actually, whose turn is it tomorrow?"

"Don't know him, and he hasn't come to introduce himself."

"Who does he work for?"

"We don't know."

"Don't forget that Gravelin has been asking each of us for a copy of our recordings. That's the least we owe him."

"That guy is a saint. How many years has he been working for Tach? It can't have been a Sunday picnic."

"No, but it must be fascinating to work for a genius."

"Genius had nothing to do with it."

"Actually, why does Gravelin want to listen to the tapes?"

"The better to know his tormentor. That, I can understand."

"I wonder how he can put up with that fat slob."

"Stop calling Tach a fat slob. Don't forget who he is."

"As far as I'm concerned, as of this morning, there is no more Tach. He will always be a fat slob and nothing more. We should never meet writers."

W ho are you? What the devil are you doing here?"

"Today is January 18, Monsieur Tach, and this is the day I've been assigned to meet you."

"Didn't your colleagues tell you that—"

"I haven't seen them. I have nothing to do with those people."

"A point in your favor. But you should have been warned."

"Your secretary, Monsieur Gravelin, had me listen to the tapes yesterday evening. I am fully aware of the circumstances."

"So you know what I think of you, and you come here all the same?"

"Yes."

"Good. Well done. That's very brave of you. And now you can leave."

"No."

"You've pulled off your stunt—what more do you need? Do you want me to sign a certificate for you?"

"No, Monsieur Tach, I really would like to speak to you."

"Listen, this is very amusing, but there are limits to my patience. The prank is finished: now out you go."

"It's out of the question. I was given permission by Monsieur Gravelin, just like all the other journalists. So I'm staying."

"That Gravelin is a traitor. I told him to tell all those women's magazines to go to hell."

"I don't work for a women's magazine."

"What? Are you telling me men's magazines now hire females?"

"It's nothing new, Monsieur Tach."

"Well, shit! What next! If they start hiring females, they'll end up hiring Negroes, and Arabs, and Iraqis!"

"And this is a Nobel Prize winner saying such tactful things?"

"Nobel Prize for literature, not Nobel Peace Prize, thank God."

"Thank God indeed."

"Madame is playing the fine wit?"

"Mademoiselle."

"Mademoiselle? I'm not surprised, with your ugly face. And sticky, on top of it! No wonder no man will have you as a wife."

"You're a few wars behind, Monsieur Tach. Nowadays, some women prefer to remain single."

"Well, I never! Why don't you just say you can't find anyone who'll screw you?"

"That, monsieur, is my business."

"Oh yes, it's your private life, now isn't it?"

"Exactly. If you think it's funny to go around telling everyone that you're a virgin, you're well within your rights. Other people are not obliged to imitate you."

"Who do you think you are to judge me, you ugly insolent unfuckable little shit face?"

"Monsieur Tach, I'm going to give you two minutes, with my watch in my hand, to apologize for what you have just said. If by the end of the two minutes you have not apologized, I will go out the door and leave you to stew in your disgusting apartment."

For a split second, the fat man seemed to be struggling for air.

"Impertinent bitch! It's pointless looking at your watch: you can stay here for two years, I will never apologize to you. You're the one who has to apologize to me. And besides, what gave you the idea I might want you to stay here? I have told you to leave the premises at least twice since you entered. So don't bother waiting until the two minutes are over, you're wasting your time. There's the door! There's the door, do you hear me?"

She pretended not to hear. She went on looking at her watch, inscrutably. What could be shorter than two minutes? And yet, two minutes can seem endless when they are being painstakingly measured in a deadly silence. The old man's indignation had time to change into stupor.

"Well, the two minutes are over. Farewell, Monsieur Tach, delighted to have met you."

She stood up and headed toward the door.

"Don't leave. I order you to stay."

"Do you have something to tell me?"

"Sit down."

"It's too late to apologize, Monsieur Tach. You've passed the deadline."

"Stay, goddammit."

"Farewell."

She opened the door.

"I'm sorry, do you hear me? I'm sorry!"

"I told you it was too late."

"For Christ's sake, this is the first time in my life I've ever said I was sorry."

"No doubt that is why your apology is so poorly formulated."

"Are you saying there is something wrong with my apology?"

"There are even several things wrong with your apology. First of all, it has come too late: you must understand that tardy apologies lose half of their virtues. And then, if you spoke our language properly, you would know that you don't say, 'I'm sorry,' you say, 'I apologize,' or, even better, 'Please forgive me,' or better still, 'Please accept my apologies.' But the best of all is, 'I beg you please to accept my humble apologies.'"

"What hypocritical gobbledygook!"

"Hypocritical or not, I am leaving this very instant if you do not present your apology in due form."

"I beg you please to accept my humble apologies."

"Mademoiselle."

"I beg you please to accept my humble apologies, Mademoiselle. Are you happy now?"

"Not at all. Did you hear the tone of your voice? You would use the same tone of voice to ask me what brand of lingerie I wear."

"What brand of lingerie do you wear?"

"Farewell, Monsieur Tach."

She opened the door again. The fat man cried out, his voice filled with urgency, "I beg you please to accept my humble apologies, Mademoiselle."

"That's better. Next time, make it snappier. To punish you for your slowness, I order you to tell me why you don't want me to go."

"What, you haven't finished yet?"

"No. I feel I deserve a perfect apology. By restricting yourself to a simple formula, you were not very credible. In order to convince me, you have to justify yourself, you have to make me want to forgive you—because I haven't forgiven you yet, that would be too easy."

"You're going too far!"

"You have the nerve to say such a thing to me?"

"Go fuck yourself."

"Fine."

She opened the door once again.

"I don't want you to leave because I'm bored shitless! I've been bored for twenty-four years!"

"Ah-hah."

"You should be happy, you'll be able to write in your rag that Prétextat Tach it is a poor old man who's been bored for twenty-four years. You'll be able to throw me to the rabble, for their odious commiseration."

"Dear monsieur, I knew very well that you were bored. You're not telling me anything new."

"You're bluffing. How could you have known?"

"There were certain contradictions, unmistakable signs. I listened to the other journalists' recordings together with Monsieur Gravelin. You said that your secretary had organized the interviews with the press against your will. Monsieur Gravelin asserted the contrary: he told me how pleased you were at the idea of being interviewed."

"Traitor!"

"It's nothing to be ashamed of, Monsieur Tach. I found you rather to my liking when I heard that."

"I don't give a shit whether I'm to your liking or not."

"And yet you don't want me to leave. What sort of entertainment are you expecting from me?"

"I'm really in a mood to piss you off. I can't think of anything more entertaining."

"I'm delighted to hear that. And you imagine that that will make me want to stay?"

"One of the greatest writers of the century gives you the enormous honor of telling you he needs you, and that's not enough for you?"

"Maybe you'd like to see me weep with joy and wash your feet with my tears?"

"Yes, I think I'd rather like that. I like to see people crawling at my feet."

"In that case, don't retain me any longer: that's not my style."

"Stay: you're tough, and that amuses me. Since you don't seem to have any intention of forgiving me, let's make a bet, all right? I'll wager you that by the end of the interview, I'll have forced you to give back your ill-gotten gains, just like your predecessors. You like bets, don't you?"

"I don't like gratuitous betting. There has to be something at stake."

"Ah, so you're interested, huh? Is it money you want?"

"No."

"Oh, Mademoiselle is above such base considerations?"

"Not at all. But if I wanted money, I would have looked for someone richer than you. It's something else I want from you."

"It wouldn't be my virginity?"

"You are obsessed with your virginity. No, I'd really have to be desperate to entertain such a horrible prospect."

"Thank you. So what is it you want?"

"You said something about crawling. I suggest identical stakes for both of us: if I crack, I'm the one who'll crawl at your feet, but if you crack, you'll crawl at my feet. I like to see people crawling at my feet, too."

"It's touching that you think you might be able to measure up to me."

"It seems to me I already won a first round just now."

"My poor child, you call that a first round? That was nothing but adorable preliminaries."

"At the end of which you were crushed."

"That's as may be. But for your victory you had at your disposal one very dissuasive argument, which you now no longer have."

"Oh, yes?"

"Yes, your argument was that you would leave. And now you no longer can, the stakes are too tempting. I saw the way your eyes shone at the thought of me crawling at your feet. The prospect is too appealing to you now. You won't leave before the end of the wager."

"You may regret it."

"I may. In the meantime I think I shall have some fun. I love squashing people, I love getting the better of anyone who's the lackey of bad faith—all of you, that is. And there is one exercise that really brings me extreme pleasure: humiliating pretentious airhead females like yourself."

"As for me, my preferred entertainment is to take the wind out of obese self-satisfied airbags."

"What you just said is so typical of your day and age. Does this mean I'm dealing with someone who churns out slogans?"

"Have no fear, Monsieur Tach: you too, with your reactionary spitefulness and everyday racism, are typical of our day and age. You take pride in thinking you're an anachronism, don't you? Well you're not, not at all. Historically, you're not even original: every generation has had its prophet of doom, its sacred monster whose glory was founded solely on the terror he inspired in naïve souls. Do I need to tell you how fragile that glory is, and that you will be forgotten? You are right to say that no one reads you. Nowadays, your crassness and insults may remind people that you exist; but once your shouts fall silent, no one will even remember you because no one will read you. And so much the better."

"What a delicious little morsel of eloquence, Mademoiselle! Where the devil were you educated? This mixture of pathetic aggression and Ciceronian flights of oratory—all carefully nuanced, so to speak, with little touches of Hegel and amateur sociology: what a masterpiece."

"Sir, may I remind you that, wager or no wager, I am still a journalist. Everything you say is being recorded."

"Fantastic. We are enriching Western thought with its most brilliant dialectic."

"Dialectic, isn't that the word everyone drags out when they've run out of anything else to say?"

"Well put. The joker of the drawing room."

"Am I to conclude that you've already run out of things to tell me?"

"I never have had anything to tell you, Mademoiselle. When you are as bored as I am and have been for twenty-four years, you have nothing to say to people. If you nevertheless aspire to their company, it is in the hopes of being entertained, if not by their wit, at least by their stupidity. So do something, entertain me."

"I don't know if I'll manage to entertain you, but I am certain I shall manage to disturb you."

"Disturb me! My poor child, my respect for you has just dropped below zero. Disturb me! Well, you could have come out with something worse, you could have said disturb, full stop. What era does that intransitive use of the verb disturb date from? May 1968? It wouldn't surprise me, it reeks of little Molotov cocktails and police barricades, a nice little revolution for well-fed students, and bright little futures for young men of means. Wanting to 'disturb' means wanting to 're-examine everything,' to 'raise consciousness'—and no pronouns, please, it sounds so much more intelligent, and then it's very practical because, basically, it enables you not to specify what you would be incapable of specifying in the first place."

"Why are you wasting your time telling me this? I already used a pronoun: I said 'disturb *you*.'"

"Yeah. That's not much better. My poor child, you would have made a perfect social worker. The funniest thing is the foolish pride of people who declare that they want to disturb: they speak to you with all the smugness of budding messiahs. Because they're on a mission, aren't they! Well then, go ahead, raise my consciousness, disturb me, let's have a good laugh."

"It's extraordinary, I'm entertaining you already."

"I'm a good audience. Go on."

"All right. Just now you said that you had nothing to tell me. It's not reciprocal."

"Let me guess. What might a little female like you have to say to me? That women are not portrayed favorably in my work? That without women, men will never achieve fulfillment?"

"Wrong."

"Well, maybe you'd like to know who does housework here?"

"Why not? It will give you the opportunity to be interesting for a change."

"Go ahead, provoke, it's the weapon of mediocre people. Well, I would have you know that a Portuguese woman comes every Thursday afternoon to clean my apartment and take my dirty laundry. There you have at least one woman who has respectable employment."

"In your ideology, women stay at home with a broom and a dust-rag, is that it?"

"In my ideology, women don't exist."

"Better and better. The Nobel committee must have had a serious sunstroke the day they chose you."

"For once, we agree. This Nobel Prize was a high point in the history of misunderstandings. To give me the Nobel Prize for literature is equivalent to giving the Nobel Peace prize to Saddam Hussein."

"Don't brag. Saddam is more famous than you are."

"That's normal, no one reads me. If people read me, I would cause more harm and therefore be more famous than Saddam."

"But the fact remains that no one reads you. How do you explain this universal refusal to read you?"

"An instinct for self-preservation. An immune-system reflex."

"You always come up with explanations that are flattering for you. And what if people did not read you simply because you are boring?"

"Boring? What an exquisite euphemism. Why don't you say a pain in the ass!"

"Because I don't think it's necessary to resort to bad language. But don't dodge the question, monsieur."

"Am I boring? I will give you a reply that is resplendent with good faith: I have no idea. Of all the inhabitants on the planet, I am the least well situated to know. Kant surely thought that the *Critique of Pure Reason* was a fascinating book, and that wasn't his fault: he had his nose in it. Consequently I feel obliged, Mademoiselle, to redirect my question to you baldly: am I boring? As silly as you may be, your reply will be more interesting than mine, even if you haven't read me, a matter about which I have many doubts."

"You are wrong. Sitting before you is one of the rare human beings who has read all twenty-two of your novels, without skipping a single line."

The fat man sat there speechless for forty seconds.

"Bravo. I like people who are capable of such enormous lies."

"Sorry to disappoint you, it's the truth. I've read everything you've ever written."

"With someone holding a gun to your head?"

"Of my own free will—no, of my own free desire."

"That's impossible. If you had read everything I've written, you would not be the person I see before me."

"And who do you see before you?"

"I see an insignificant little female."

"And do you think you can see what is going on in the head of this insignificant little female?"

"What, is there something going on in your head? *Tota mulier in utero.*"

"I regret to inform you, I did not read you with my belly. So you will be subjected to my opinions. There's no way around it."

"Go ahead, let's see what you mean by 'opinion.'"

"First and foremost, to respond to your first question, I was not bored for a single moment reading your twenty-two novels."

"That's strange. I would think that reading something without understanding it would be deadly boring."

"And what about writing without understanding, is that boring?"

"Are you suggesting that I do not understand my own books?"

"I would say, rather, that your books are overflowing with a desire to show off and bluff. And that is part of their charm: while I was reading you, I was aware of a continuous alternation between passages that were deep with meaning and interludes that were absolute bluff—I say absolute because they were bluffing the author just as much as the reader. I can imagine the jubilation you must have felt while filling these brilliantly hollow, outrageously solemn interludes with an appearance of depth and cogency. For someone who is such a virtuoso, it must have been exquisite recreation."

"What the hell are you going on about?"

"I found it exquisite. To discover so much bad faith in the words of a writer who claims to be at war with bad faith is utterly charming. It would have been irritating if your perfidy had been homogeneous. But to go back and forth between good and bad faith the way you did was a brilliant display of dishonesty."

"And do you think you're capable of differentiating between the two, pretentious little female?"

"What could be simpler? Every time a passage made me burst out laughing, I could tell that you were bluffing. And I thought it was very clever: an excellent strategy, using bad faith and intellectual terrorism to fight against bad faith, being even more underhand than your adversary. Maybe too excellent, in fact, because it's too refined for such a vulgar enemy. It will come as no news to you, but Machiavellianism rarely hits the bull's eye: sledgehammers do a better job at crushing than subtle mechanisms do."

"You say that I am bluffing: well, I make a paltry bluffer compared to you, claiming you've read all my novels the way you do."

"Everything that was available, yes. Question me, if you want to make sure."

"Uh-huh, just like Tintin addicts: 'What is the license plate number of the red Volvo in *The Calculus Affair*?' It's grotesque. Don't expect me to dishonor my works in such a fashion."

"Well, how can I convince you, then?"

"You can't. You will not convince me."

"In that case, I have nothing to lose."

"With me, you never have *had* anything to lose. You've been doomed from the start because of your sex."

"Incidentally, I indulged in a little survey of your female characters."

"Here we go. God knows."

"Earlier on, you said that according to your belief system, women do not exist. I find it astonishing that a man who professes such a creed has created so many women on paper. I won't go over all of them, but I counted roughly forty-six female characters in your work."

"And what is that supposed to prove?"

"It proves that women do exist in your ideology: a first contradiction. And you will see, there are others."

"Oh! Mademoiselle is on the hunt for contradictions! I would have you know, Mademoiselle Schoolmarm, that Prétextat Tach has raised contradiction to the level of a fine art. Can you imagine anything more elegant, more subtle, more disconcerting, or more acute than my system of self-contradiction? And now along comes a silly little goose—all that's missing is a pair of glasses on her nose—triumphantly announcing to me that she has uncovered a few unfortunate contradictions in my work! Isn't it marvelous having such discerning readers?"

"I never said that the contradiction was unfortunate."

"No, but it's obvious that's what you were thinking."

"I'm in a better position than you to know what I am thinking."

"That remains to be seen."

"And, as it happens, I thought the contradiction was interesting."

"Good Lord."

"Forty-six female characters, as I was saying."

"For your calculations to be of any interest whatsoever, you should have counted how many male characters there are, too, my child."

"I did."

"Such presence of mind."

"One hundred and sixty-three male characters."

"My poor girl, if you did not inspire so much pity, I would readily laugh at such a disproportion."

"Beware of pity."

"Ooh! She's read Zweig! How cultured she is! You see, my dear, the peasants who resemble me go no further than Montherlant, who seems to be cruelly lacking from your reading. I pity women, so I hate them, and vice versa."

"Since you have such healthy feelings toward our sex, please explain why you created forty-six female characters."

"It's out of the question: you are the one who is going to explain it to me. I would not forego such entertainment for anything on earth."

"It is not up to me to explain your work to you. However, I can share a few remarks."

"Please do."

"I'll give them to you off the top of my head. You have written books without any women: there is *Apology of Dyspepsia*, of course—"

"Why 'of course'?"

"Because it contains no characters at all, obviously."

"So it's true you have read me, at least in part."

"Nor are there any women in *The Solvent, Pearls for a Massacre, Buddha in a Glass of Water, Assault on Ugliness, Total Disaster, Death and Then Some*, or even—and this is more astonishing—in *Poker, Women, and Other People*."

"What exquisite subtlety on my part."

"So that makes eight novels without women. Twenty-two

minus eight makes fourteen. So there are fourteen novels sharing out the forty-six female characters."

"Isn't science wonderful."

"Naturally the characters are not evenly spread out among the fourteen remaining books."

"Why 'naturally'? I cannot stand all these 'naturally's and 'of course's you resort to when speaking of my books, as if my oeuvre were so very predictable, with transparent inner workings."

"It is precisely because your oeuvre is so unpredictable that I used the term 'naturally.'"

"No sophistry, please."

"The absolute record for female characters is held by *Gratuitous Rapes Between the Wars*, where there are twenty-three women."

"There's a reason for that."

"Forty-six minus twenty-three equals twenty-three. Which leaves us with thirteen novels and twenty-three women."

"Admirable statistics."

"You wrote four monogynous novels, if you will allow me such an incongruous neologism."

"But can you yourself allow it?"

"They are: *Prayer on Breaking and Entering*, *The Sauna and Other Luxuries*, *The Prose of Epilation*, and *Dying without Adverbs*."

"Which leaves us with?"

"Nine novels and nineteen women."

"And how are they divided up?"

"*Dirty People*: three women. All the other books are dygynous: *Crucifixion Made Easy*, *The Disorder of the Garter*, *Urbi and Orbi*, *Slaves in the Oasis*, *Membranes*, *Three Boudoirs*, *Concomitant Grace*—wait, there's one missing."

"No, you've named them all."

"Are you sure?"

"Yes, you've learned your lesson well."

"I'm convinced there's one missing. Let me count over from the beginning."

"Oh, no, you're not going to start all over!"

"I have to, otherwise my statistics won't tally."

"I will give you my absolution."

"Never mind, I'll start over. Have you got a piece of paper and a pencil?"

"No."

"Please, Monsieur Tach, help me, we'll save time."

"I told you not to start over again. You are an utter bore with all your lists!"

"Then help me not to have to start over again, and tell me the title that is missing."

"But I have no idea. I've already forgotten all the titles you listed."

"You forget your own work?"

"Naturally. You'll see, when you get to be eighty-three years old."

"But still, there are some of your novels that you cannot have forgotten."

"No doubt, but which ones exactly?"

"It's not up to me to tell you."

"What a pity. Your judgment is so amusing."

"I'm delighted. And now, please be quiet a moment. Let's see: *Apology for Dyspepsia*, that makes one, *The Solvent*—"

"Are you having me on or what?"

"—makes two. *Pearls for a Massacre*, three."

"Do you have any earplugs on you?"

"Do you have the missing title?"

"No."

"Never mind. *Buddha in a Glass of Water*, four. *Assault on Ugliness*, five."

"165. 28. 3925. 424."

"You're not about to confuse me. *Total Disaster*, six. *Death and Then Some*, seven."

"Would you like a toffee?"

"No. *Poker, Women, and Other People*, eight. *Gratuitous Rapes Between the Wars*, nine."

"Would you like a Brandy Alexander?"

"Be quiet. *Prayer on Breaking and Entering*, ten."

"You're watching your weight, aren't you? I was sure of it. Don't you think you're thin enough as it is?"

"*The Sauna and Other Luxuries*, eleven."

"I expected just such an answer."

"*The Prose of Epilation*, twelve."

"My my, this is crazy, you're reciting them in exactly the same order as the first time."

"You see yourself that you have an excellent memory. *Dying without Adverbs*, thirteen."

"You mustn't exaggerate. But why don't you list them in chronological order?"

"You even remember them in chronological order? *Dirty People*, fourteen. *Crucifixion Made Easy*, fifteen."

"Do me a favor, stop there."

"On one condition: give me the missing title. Your memory is far too good to have forgotten it."

"And yet I have. Amnesia tends to be incoherent."

"*The Disorder of the Garter*, sixteen."

"Are you going to go on like this for long?"

"Just long enough to stimulate your memory."

"My memory? You did say 'my' memory?"

"Indeed."

"Am I to understand that you yourself have not forgotten the novel in question?"

"How could I have forgotten it?"

"But why don't you just say it, then?"

"I want to hear you say it."

"But I'm telling you, once again, I don't remember it."

"I don't believe you. You could have forgotten all the others, but not that one."

"What's so extraordinary about it, then?"

"You know perfectly well."

"No. I'm an unwitting genius?"

"Make me laugh."

"Besides, if that novel was so fabulous, someone would have already mentioned it. And no one ever has. When people talk about my work, they always refer to the same four books."

"You know very well that that doesn't prove a thing."

"Oh, I see. Mademoiselle is a drawing room snob. You're the type who exclaims, 'Dear friend, have you read Proust? No, no, not *Remembrance of Things Past,* don't be vulgar. I mean the article he published in 1904 in *Le Figaro* . . .'"

"So let's agree that I'm a snob. The missing title, please."

"I'm afraid I don't like it."

"Which confirms my assumption."

"Your assumption? Well, I never."

"Fine. Since you refuse to cooperate, I will have to start my list all over again—I don't remember where I left off."

"You don't need to repeat your litany, you know the missing title."

"Alas, I fear I've forgotten it again. *Apology for Dyspepsia,* one."

"One more word and I'll strangle you, crippled though I may be."

"Strangle? The choice of the verb is telling."

"Would you prefer I gave you a rabbit punch?"

"This time, monsieur, you will not succeed in avoiding the subject. So talk to me about strangling."

"What? I wrote a book with that title?"

"Not exactly."

"Listen, you're getting downright exasperating with all your riddles. Tell me the title and let's get it over with."

"I'm in no hurry to get it over with. I'm having too much fun."

"Well, you're the only one."

"Which makes the situation all the more pleasant. But let's not get off the subject. Talk to me about strangling, my good man."

"I have nothing to say on the matter."

"Oh, no? Why were you threatening me, then?"

"I just said it, well, the way I would have said, 'Go fly a kite!'"

"Yes. And yet, what a coincidence: you preferred to threaten me with strangling. How strange."

"What are you getting at? Maybe you have a thing about Freudian slips? That's all I need."

"I didn't use to believe in Freudian slips. But as of a minute ago, I've become a believer."

"I didn't use to believe in the efficiency of verbal torture. And now as of these last few minutes I've started to believe in it."

"You flatter me. But let's put our cards on the table, all right? I have plenty of time, and until you dig that missing title out of your memory, and until you speak to me about strangling, I will not leave you alone."

"Aren't you ashamed, hounding a crippled old man who is obese, and destitute, and sick?"

"I don't know what that is, shame."

"Yet another virtue that your teachers neglected to inculcate you with."

"Monsieur Tach, you don't know what shame is, either."

"That's normal. I have no reason to be ashamed."

"Didn't you say that your books are harmful?"

"Precisely: I would be ashamed if I had *not* harmed humankind."

"As it happens, I'm not interested in humankind."

"Nor should you be: humankind is not interesting."

"But individuals are interesting, aren't they?"

"Indeed, they are so rare."

"Talk to me about an individual that you have known."

"Well, there is Céline, for example."

"Oh, no, not Céline."

"What? Is he not interesting enough for Mademoiselle?"

"Talk to me about a flesh-and-blood individual that you have known, with whom you have lived, spoken, etc."

"The nurse?"

"No, not the nurse. Come on, you know who I mean. You know perfectly well."

"I have no idea, you irritating little bitch."

"I'm going to tell you a little story, which might help your senile brain to retrieve its memories."

"Go right ahead. Since I am not going to be allowed to speak for some time, I request permission to go get some toffees. I sorely need them, with all the torment your are subjecting me to."

"Permission granted."

The novelist placed a huge square toffee in his mouth.

"My story begins with an astonishing discovery. Journalists are creatures who are completely devoid of scruples, that you know. Therefore, I rummaged around in your past without consulting you, because you would have forbidden it. I can see you smiling and I know what you're thinking: that you covered all your tracks, that you are the last representative of your family, that you have never had any friends—in short, that I would not be able to dig up any information about your past. You are mistaken, dear sir. You must beware of underhand witnesses. You must beware of the places where you have lived. They speak. I see you are laughing once again. Yes, your childhood château burned down sixty-five years ago. A strange fire, actually, that was never explained."

"How did you hear about the château?" asked the fat man in a languid voice sticky with toffee.

"Oh, that was very easy. Elementary research in registers and archives—easy stuff for journalists. You see, Monsieur Tach, I didn't wait until January 10 to become interested in you. I've been studying your case for years now."

"How industrious you are! You must have thought, 'The old man won't live much longer, let's be ready for the day he dies,' is that it?"

"Stop talking and chewing that toffee at the same time, it's disgusting. Let me get back to my story. My research was long and hazardous, but not difficult. I eventually found the trace of the last members of the Tach family known to the public: there is the record of the death in 1909 of Casimir and Célestine Tach, who drowned in the tide at Mont Saint-Michel, where the young couple had gone on a trip. They'd been married for two years and they left behind a one-year-old child—I'll let you guess who that was. On learning of the tragic death of their only son, Casimir Tach's parents died of sorrow. After that, there was only one Tach left, Prétextat. It was more difficult for me to follow your own trajectory. I had the bright idea of looking up your mother's maiden name and I learned that, while your father came from a little-known family, Célestine was born the marquise de Planèze de Saint-Sulpice, a branch that has now died out, not to be confused with the de Planèze counts and countesses . . ."

"Do you intend to tell me the history of a family that is not my own?"

"You're right, I'm getting off the subject. Let's get back to the Planèze de Saint-Sulpice family: there were not many of them left by 1909, but their background was impeccable and they were well respected. When they learned of their daughter's death, the marquis and marquise decided to take charge of their orphaned grandson, and that is how you came to live in the château at Saint-Sulpice at one year of age. You were pampered not only by your nurse and your grandparents, but also by your uncle and aunt, Cyprien and Cosima de Planèze, your mother's brother and sister-in-law."

"These genealogical details are so interesting they're taking my breath away."

"Don't they indeed? Let's see what you will have to say about that which is still to come?"

"What? You haven't finished yet?"

"Certainly not. You're not even two years old yet, and I want to tell you your life story up to the age of eighteen."

"Lord help us."

"If you had told it to me yourself, I wouldn't be obliged to do it."

"And what if I didn't feel like talking about it, huh?"

"Well, that was because you have something to hide."

"Not necessarily."

"It's too early to go into that. Now, you were a baby your family adored, despite your mother's misalliance. I've seen sketches of that château that no longer exists: it was splendid. What a dream of a childhood you must have had!"

"Do you write for that rag *Hello!* by any chance?"

"When you were two, your aunt and uncle gave birth to their only child, Léopoldine de Planèze de Saint-Sulpice."

"It makes you foam at the mouth, a name like that, doesn't it? Not the sort of name you could ever have."

"Yes, but at least I'm alive."

"For all the good it does you."

"May I go on, or do you want me to let you do the talking? Your memory must be resuscitated by now."

"Go on, please, I'm having a wonderful time."

"So much the better, because we're a long way from the end, still. So, as I was saying, they gave you the only thing that was missing: some company your own age. You never had to experience the dreary days of a friendless only child; naturally, even though you didn't go to school and didn't have any classmates, you had something much better: an adorable little cousin. You became inseparable. Do you want to know how I came upon these details?"

"With the help of your imagination, I suppose."

"In part. But an imagination needs fuel, Monsieur Tach, and I owe the fuel to you."

"Stop continually interrupting yourself and tell me about my childhood, it's bringing tears to my eyes."

"Scoff all you like, monsieur. There will be plenty more to bring tears to your eyes. Your childhood was far too beautiful. You had everything anyone can dream of, and then some: a château, a huge estate with lakes and forests, horses, incredible material ease, an adoptive family who cherished you, a tutor who was not at all authoritarian and who was often on sick leave, loving servants, and above all, you had Léopoldine."

"Tell me the truth: you're not a journalist. You are looking for material to write a romance novel."

"A romance novel? We'll see about that. Back to my story. Of course, in 1914, there was the war, but children find a way to live with war, particularly rich kids. Viewed from your paradise, the conflict seemed insignificant, and it scarcely ruffled the waters of the long, slow flow of your happiness."

"My dear, you are a peerless storyteller."

"Not as good as you."

"Continue."

"The years hardly went by. Childhood does not move at a very rapid pace. What is a year for an adult? For a child, a year is a century, and for you these centuries were made of gold and silver. The lawyers regularly invoked an unhappy childhood as an attenuating circumstance. But in delving into your past, I realized that too happy a childhood could also serve as an attenuating circumstance."

"Why are you trying to give me the benefit of attenuating circumstances? I don't need them at all."

"We'll see. You and Léopoldine were inseparable. You could not live without each other."

"Loving cousins: that's as old as the world."

"When two people are as close as you two were, can one even still speak of loving cousins?"

"Brother and sister, if you prefer."

"Incestuous brother and sister, then."

"Are you shocked? It happens in the best of families. Which just goes to show."

"I think it's up to you to tell me the rest of the story."

"I'll do no such thing."

"Do you really want me to go on?"

"I would be much obliged."

"I'm not asking you to be obliged, but if I were to go on with my story from the point that I've reached, it would be only a pale and mediocre paraphrase of the most beautiful, unusual, and least known of your novels."

"I adore pale, mediocre paraphrases."

"Then too bad, you asked for it. Am I right, then?"

"About what?"

"To have classified that novel among your books with two female characters and not three female characters."

"You are absolutely correct, dear lady."

"In that case, I have nothing left to fear. The rest is literature, isn't it?"

"The rest is indeed my work alone. In those days, I had no paper other than my own life, no ink other than my own blood."

"Or that of others."

"She was not an 'other.'"

"Then who was she?"

"That is something I never found out; but she was not an

other, that much is certain. I am still waiting for your paraphrase, dear lady."

"Indeed. The years went by, and they were good years, too
good, perhaps. You and Léopoldine had never known any
other life, yet you were both aware that it was not usual, and
that you were exceedingly lucky. In the depths of your paradise,
you began to feel what you call 'the anxiety of the chosen few,'
which consists of the following: 'How long can such perfection
last?' This anxiety, like all anxieties, fueled your euphoria to the
extreme, while leaving it dangerously fragile—more and more
dangerously. A few more years went by. You were fourteen
years old, your cousin was twelve. You had reached the culmi-
nating point of childhood, the moment that Tournier refers to
as the 'full maturity of childhood.' You had been shaped by a
dream life, and you were dream children. No one had ever told
you as much, but you were becoming obscurely aware that a terrible degradation lay in wait, about to attack your perfect
bodies and your equally perfect humor, to turn you into pimply,
tormented teenagers. I suspect you had arrived at the origin, by
then, of the insane plot that followed."

"Here we go, you're already trying to exonerate my accom-
plice."

"I don't see why I shouldn't. It was your idea, was it not?"

"Yes, but there was nothing criminal about it."

"Not to begin with, no, but it became criminal because of
the consequences and, above all, because, sooner or later, it
would prove totally unworkable."

"Later, as it happened."

"Let's not get ahead of ourselves. You were fourteen, Léopoldine was twelve. She was devoted to you, and you could make
her believe anything."

"It wasn't just anything."

"No, it was worse. You convinced her that puberty was the
worst of all evils, but that it was avoidable."

"It is."

"You still believe that?"

"I've never stopped believing it."

"So you've always been insane."

"From my point of view, I am the only one who has always been of sound mind."

"Naturally. At the age of fourteen, you were already so sound of mind that you solemnly swore you would never become an adolescent. Your hold over your cousin was so strong that you made her take an oath identical to your own."

"Adorable, isn't it?"

"That depends. For you were already Prétextat Tach, and along with your grandiose preachings there were a number of dispositions that would prove punitive in the event of perjury. To state things more clearly, you swore, and you made Léopoldine swear, that if either of you betrayed the oath and became pubescent, he or she would be killed by the other one, purely and simply."

"A mere fourteen years of age, and already the soul of a Titan."

"I suppose that many children have dreamt up ways to remain eternal children, with varying but always precarious degrees of success. But the two of you seemed to have succeeded. It is true that you displayed an uncommon amount of determination. And you, the Titan in the matter, came up with all sorts of pseudoscientific measures designed to make your bodies unsuited for adolescence."

"Not so pseudoscientific as all that, because they worked."

"We'll see about that. I wonder how you survived such treatment."

"We were happy."

"At such a cost! Where the devil did your brain go to find such twisted ideas? Well, I suppose you had the excuse that you were only fourteen."

"If I had to do it all over again, I would."

"Today, you have the excuse that you're senile."

"I suppose that means I've always been senile, or puerile, because I have never changed my ideas."

"That doesn't surprise me, coming from you. Already in 1922 you were crazy. *Ex nihilo* you created what you called 'a hygiene of eternal childhood'—at the time, the word covered every domain of mental and physical health: hygiene was an ideology. The one you devised was so unhealthy that it would better deserve the name anti-hygiene."

"On the contrary, it was very healthy."

"You were convinced that puberty did its evil work during sleep, so you decreed that you must not sleep anymore, or at least not more than two hours a day. You thought the ideal way to hang on to childhood would be an aquatic life, so you and Léopoldine spent entire days and nights swimming in the lakes on the estate, sometimes even in winter. You ate a strict minimum. Some foods were forbidden, and others were recommended, by virtue of principles that seem utterly fantastical: any food considered too 'adult' was prohibited, such as *canard à l'orange* or lobster bisque, or any food that was black in color. On the other hand, you recommended mushrooms, not poisonous ones, but some that were not considered fit for consumption, either, such as puffballs, and when they were in season, you stuffed yourselves with them. To keep from sleeping, you got hold of an excessively strong tea from Kenya—you'd heard your grandmother speaking ill of it, and you would brew it black as ink and drink impressive quantities of it, while administering identical doses to your cousin."

"Who was fully consenting."

"Let's just say, rather, that she loved you."

"And I loved her, too."

"In your way."

"Do you find something wrong with my way?"

"That's an understatement."

"Maybe you think that other people are better at it? I know of nothing more vile than what they call loving. Do you know what loving is for them? Taking an unfortunate woman and getting her pregnant, and making her into an ugly servant: that is what these alleged human beings of my sex call loving."

"And now you're playing the feminist? I've never known you to be more unbelievable."

"You are lamentably stupid, I do declare. Feminism and what I just said are poles apart."

"Why can't you just try to be clear for once?"

"But I'm being crystal clear! You're the one who refuses to admit that my way of loving is the most beautiful."

"My opinion on the subject is of no interest whatsoever. However, I would like to know what Léopoldine thought about it."

"Thanks to me, Léopoldine was the happiest."

"The happiest what? The happiest of women? Of madwomen? Of sick people? Of casualties?"

"You are completely beside the point. Thanks to me, she was the happiest of children."

"Of children? At the age of fifteen?"

"Absolutely. At an age when women become dreadful—pimply, stinky, hairy, titty, intellectual, spiteful, and stupid, with prominent hips and protruding asses—in short, women. At that sinister age, as I was saying, Léopoldine was the most beautiful, happy, illiterate, wise child—the most childish of children, and totally thanks to me. Thanks to me, the girl that I loved was spared the torture of becoming a woman. I defy you to find a more beautiful love than that."

"Are you absolutely sure that your cousin did not want to become a woman?"

"How could she have wanted such a thing? She was far too intelligent for that."

"I'm not asking you to reply with conjectures. I'm asking

you whether, yes or no, she gave you her consent, and whether, yes or no, she said to you in no uncertain terms: 'Prétextat, I would rather die than leave childhood behind.'"

"She didn't need to tell me in no uncertain terms. It was self-evident."

"Just as I thought: she never gave you her consent."

"Allow me to repeat that it was pointless. I knew what she wanted."

"You knew, above all, what *you* wanted."

"She and I wanted the same thing."

"Naturally."

"What are you trying to insinuate, you shitty little bitch? Are you claiming to know Léopoldine better than I do?"

"The more I talk to you, the more I believe I do."

"When I hear such rubbish I almost wish I were deaf. I'm going to tell you something that you surely don't know, bloody female: no one, do you understand, no one knows a person better than their assassin."

"Ah-hah. At last. Are you prepared to confess?"

"Confess? I have nothing to confess, because you already knew that I killed her."

"Well, would you believe that I did have my lingering doubts? It's hard to convince oneself that a Nobel Prize winner could be an assassin."

"What? Didn't you know that assassins are the very people who have the greatest chance of receiving a Nobel Prize? Just look at Kissinger, Gorbachev . . ."

"Yes, but you won the Nobel Prize for literature."

"Precisely! Nobel Peace Prize winners are often assassins, but the literature winners are always assassins."

"It's impossible to have a serious discussion with you."

"I've never been more serious."

"Maeterlinck, Tagore, Pirandello, Mauriac, Hemingway, Pasternak, Kawabata—all assassins?"

"You didn't know?"

"No."

"You'll have learned a few things from me, then."

"May I know your source of information?"

"Prétextat Tach doesn't need sources of information. Sources of information are for ordinary people."

"I see."

"No, you don't see a thing. You go digging into my past, you rifle through my archives, and then you are surprised to come upon a murder. What would be astonishing is anything to the contrary. If you had gone to the trouble of combing through the archives of those other Nobel Prize winners with as much diligence, no doubt you would have discovered stacks of murders. Otherwise, no one would have ever given them the Nobel Prize."

"You accused the previous journalist of reversing causality. But you don't reverse causality, you merely cut in front of it."

"I want to give you ample warning that if you try to confront me on my own territory where logic is concerned, you don't stand a chance."

"Given what you qualify as logic, I don't doubt it. But I didn't come here to debate with you."

"So why did you come, then?"

"To find out whether you really were the murderer. Thank you for illuminating my last doubts: you fell for my bluff."

The fat man gave a long, hideous laugh.

"Your bluff! That's a good one! You think you can bluff me?"

"I have every reason to believe I can, because I already have."

"Poor, pathetic, pretentious goose. Let me tell you that bluffing is extortion. But you haven't extorted anything for me, because I've told you the truth right from the start. Why should I hide the fact I'm a murderer? I have nothing to fear from the law, I'm going to die in less than two months."

"And what about your posthumous reputation?"

"This will make it all the more grandiose. I can already see the window displays in the bookstores: 'Prétextat Tach, Nobel Prize for Murder.' My books will sell like hot cakes. My publishers will be rubbing their hands together. Believe me, this murder is an excellent affair for everyone concerned."

"Even for Léopoldine?"

"Above all for Léopoldine."

"Let's go back to 1922."

"Why not 1925?"

"You're getting ahead of yourself. You mustn't skip over those three years, they are extremely important."

"That's true. They are extremely important, so they cannot be related."

"And yet you did relate them."

"No, I wrote them."

"Let's not play with words, all right?"

"You are saying this to a writer?"

"I'm not talking to the writer, I'm talking to the assassin."

"One and the same."

"Are you sure of that?"

"Writer, assassin: two aspects of a same profession, two conjugations of a same verb."

"Which verb is that?"

"The rarest and most difficult of verbs: the verb 'to love.' Isn't it funny how school grammar books sometimes use it as an example, when it's the verb with the most incomprehensible meaning? If I were a teacher, I would replace this esoteric verb with a more accessible one."

"'To kill'?"

"'To kill' is not so easy, either. No, a trivial, ordinary verb like vote, interview, work, create . . ."

"Thank God you are not a teacher. Do you know that it's

extraordinarily difficult to make you answer a question? You have a real talent for dodging the issue, changing the subject, going off in all directions. I'm forever having to call you to order."

"I'm flattered."

"This time, you won't get off: 1922 through 1925, it's your turn to speak."

Heavy silence.

"Would you like a toffee?"

"Monsieur Tach, why don't you trust me?"

"It's not that I don't trust you. In all good faith, I do not see what else I could tell you. We were perfectly happy and divinely in love. What more could I tell you other than silly nonsense like that?"

"Let me help you."

"I fear the worst."

"Twenty-four years ago, following your literary menopause, you left one novel unfinished. Why?"

"I already explained this to one of your colleagues. Any self-respecting novelist must leave at least one novel unfinished, otherwise he's not believable."

"Do you know very many writers who publish unfinished novels during their lifetime?"

"I don't know of any. Undoubtedly I am cleverer than the others: during my lifetime I have received honors that ordinary writers enjoy only posthumously. From a struggling writer, an unfinished novel merely represents his awkwardness, his still unbridled youth; but on the part of a great, renowned writer, an unfinished novel is as chic as you get. It suggests a 'genius stopped in his tracks,' 'the Titan's crisis of angst,' 'dazzled when faced with the unspeakable,' 'the nightmare vision of a novel to come'—in short, it pays."

"Monsieur Tach, I think you haven't quite grasped my question. I wasn't asking you why you left *one* novel unfinished, but why you left *that* novel unfinished."

"Well, as I was writing, I realized that I had not yet produced the unfinished novel I required for my fame, so I looked down at my manuscript and thought, 'Why not this one?' I put down my pen and did not add another line."

"Do not expect me to believe you."

"Why not?"

"You said, 'I put down my pen and did not add another line.' You should have said, 'I put down my pen and never wrote another line.' Isn't it astonishing that after this famous, unfinished novel, you never wanted to write again, although you had been writing every day for thirty-six years?"

"I had to stop someday."

"But why that particular day?"

"Don't go looking for hidden meaning in a phenomenon as banal as old age. I was fifty-nine years old, so I retired. What could be more normal?"

"From one day to the next, not another line: you're saying old age caught up with you in one day?"

"Why not? You don't get old every day. You can spend ten, twenty years without getting old, and then suddenly, for no specific reason, you can show the weight of those twenty years in the space of two hours. You'll see, it will happen to you, too. One evening, you'll look in the mirror and think, 'My God, I've aged ten years since this morning!'"

"For no specific reason, really?"

"For no reason other than time hurrying everything to its doom."

"It's easy to blame time, Monsieur Tach. But you gave it a serious helping hand—with both hands, I'd say."

"The hand is what enables a writer to experience pleasure."

"And two hands are what enable a strangler to experience pleasure."

"Strangling is a pleasant thing, indeed."

"For the strangler, or the victim?"

"Alas, I've only ever known one of the two situations."

"Don't give up hope."

"What do you mean?"

"I have no idea. You're confusing me with all your digressions. Talk to me about the book, Monsieur Tach."

"It's out of the question, Mademoiselle. It's up to you to talk about it."

"Of everything you've ever written, this book is the one I prefer."

"Why? Because there's a château, and aristocrats, and a love story? Typical woman."

"I do like love stories, it's true. I often think that nothing beyond love is of any interest."

"Heavens above."

"Be as sarcastic as you like, you cannot deny that you are the one who wrote that book, and that it is a love story."

"If you say so."

"It is, moreover, the only love story you ever wrote."

"I'm relieved to hear it."

"Let me put my question to you again, sir: why did you leave that novel unfinished?"

"My imagination failed me, I suppose."

"Imagination? You did not need any imagination to write that book, you were relating the facts."

"What do you know? You weren't there to check on things."

"You did kill Léopoldine, didn't you?"

"Yes, but that doesn't prove that the rest is true. The rest is literature, Mademoiselle."

"Well, I believe that everything in that book is true."

"If it amuses you."

"It's not just amusing, I have good reason to think that the novel is strictly autobiographical."

"Good reason? Pray explain, so we can have a good laugh."

"Your descriptions of the château are exact, according to the archives. The characters have the same names in real life, except for you yourself, of course, but Philémon Tractatus is a transparent pseudonym, with the initials to prove it. Finally, the registers confirm that Léopoldine died in 1925."

"Archives, registers: is that what you call real life?"

"No, but the fact that you respected official facts has led me, perfectly reasonably, to deduce that you also respected a more secret truth."

"A weak argument."

"But I have others: the style, for example. An infinitely less abstract style than that of your previous novels."

"An even weaker argument. This impressionism replaces any critical judgment you might have, and can hardly serve as proof, particularly where style is concerned: slaves of your sort invariably come out with utter nonsense when the issue of a writer's style is in question."

"I have one final argument, which is all the more devastating in that it is not an argument."

"What on earth are you on about now?"

"It's not an argument, it's a photograph."

"A photograph? What of?"

"Do you know why no one has ever suspected that this novel was autobiographical? Because the main character, Philémon Tractatus, was a magnificent, slender boy with an admirable face. You weren't really lying when you told my colleagues that from the age of eighteen on, you have been ugly and obese. Let's just say that you were lying by omission, for in all the years prior to that, you were unbelievably handsome."

"How do you know?"

"I found a photograph."

"Impossible. I did not have my picture taken until 1948."

"I'm sorry, but I am forced to find your memory lacking. I discovered a photograph where on the back is written, in pencil, 'Saint-Sulpice, 1925.'"

"Show me."

"I'll show you when I'm certain that you won't try to destroy it."

"I see, you're bluffing."

"I'm not bluffing. I went on a pilgrimage to Saint-Sulpice. I regret to inform you that on the site of the former château—of which nothing remains—there is an agricultural co-op. Most of the lakes on the estate have been drained, and the valley has been transformed into a public dump. I'm sorry, but you inspire no pity in me. I questioned all the old people I could find in the area. They still remembered the château and the various marquis de Planèze de Saint-Sulpice. They even remembered the little orphan adopted by his grandparents."

"I wonder how on earth those locals could possibly remember me, I never had any contact with them."

"There are different ways of having contact. Maybe they never spoke to you, but they saw you."

"That's impossible. I never set foot outside the estate."

"But friends came to visit your grandparents, and your aunt and uncle."

"They never took any photographs."

"You're mistaken. Listen, I don't know under what circumstances the photograph was taken, nor by whom—my explanations were just hypotheses—but the fact remains that the photograph does exist. You are standing in front of the château with Léopoldine."

"With Léopoldine?"

"A ravishing child with dark hair. Who else could it be?"

"Show me that photograph."

"What will you do with it?"   ·

"Show me that photograph, I tell you."

"A very old woman in the village gave it to me. I don't know how it ended up in her hands. It doesn't matter: the identity of the two children leaves no doubt. Children, yes—even you, at

here's nothing incredible about it, it happens all the time.
As a rule, it doesn't happen so quickly."

"Ah, good, you've just confessed again."

"Huh?"

"Yes. By saying that, you have implicitly acknowledged the truth of my words. At the age of seventeen, you were indeed as I described—and unfortunately, no photograph ever captured you like that for immortality."

"I knew it! But how did you manage to describe me so well?"

"I simply paraphrased the descriptions of Philémon Tractatus in your novel. I wanted to make sure that you were just as you described your character: in order to find out, there was no other way to go about it than to bluff, since you refused to answer my questions."

"You are a filthy little muckraker."

"It's effective, raking up muck: I now know for certain that your novel is strictly autobiographical. I have every reason to be proud of myself, because I had the same elements to go on as everyone else. And yet I'm the only one who has had any inkling of the truth."

"Be my guest, act all proud."

"So allow me henceforth to ask my first question all over again: why is *Hygiene and the Assassin* an unfinished novel?"

"That's it, that's the title that was missing earlier!"

"Don't try to act all surprised. I won't give up until you answer: why is the novel unfinished?"

"You could frame the question in a more metaphysical way: why is that incompletion a novel?"

"I'm not interested in your metaphysics. Answer my question: why is the novel unfinished?"

"Hell and damnation, you piss me off! Does the novel not have the right to be unfinished?"

"Whether it has the right or not really has nothing to do with

the age of seventeen, show no signs of add
you are both very tall, thin, and gaunt, bu
long bodies are perfectly childlike. You don
ally: you look like two twelve-year-old giants.
is superb: fine features, childlike eyes, but you
in comparison with your skull. Your torso is tha
legs are lanky and interminable—worthy subject
It's enough to make me believe that your insan
hygiene actually worked, and that puffballs are a b
And you are the greatest shock of all. Totally unrecc

"If I'm so unrecognizable, how do you know tha

"Who else could it be? Besides, you have the sar
smooth, hairless skin—that is indeed the only thing y
preserved. You were so handsome, your features so pur
such delicate limbs and an asexual complexion so asexua
the order of an angel."

"Spare me your religious twaddle, would you? And show
the photograph, instead of spouting rubbish."

"How could you have changed so much? You said that at th
age of eighteen you were already as you are now, and I'm willing
to believe it—but in this case, it just makes it all the more
astounding: how could you, in less than a year, have swapped
your seraphic appearance for the bloated monster I see before
me? Not only did you triple in weight, your delicate face
became bovine, your refined features so thick as to be completely vulgar . . ."

"Have you finished insulting me?"

"You know very well that you are ugly. Besides, you constantly
use the most disgusting adjectives in referring to yourself."

"I may use them on myself with a witty turn of phrase, but I
will not allow other people to use them. Is that clear?"

"I don't give a damn whether you allow me or not. You're
horrible, that's all there is to it, and it's incredible that you could
be so horrible when you were once so handsome."

it. You were writing truth with a true purpose, so why didn't you finish the novel? After Léopoldine's murder, the story comes to an abrupt end, above a void. Would it have been so difficult to wrap it up, give it a proper ending?"

"Difficult! I would have you know, silly goose, that nothing is difficult for Prétextat Tach."

"Precisely. Which makes this abrupt non-ending all the more absurd."

"Who are you to rule on the absurdity of my decisions?"

"I'm not ruling on anything, I'm just wondering."

The old man suddenly looked like an old man, eighty-three years of age.

"You are not the only one. I too am wondering, and I cannot find the answer. I could have chosen dozens of endings for that book: either the murder itself, or the night that followed, or my physical metamorphosis, or the fire in the château, a year later . . . "

"That was your doing, the fire, wasn't it?"

"Of course. Saint-Sulpice had become intolerable without Léopoldine. Moreover, I was getting annoyed with my family's suspicions about me. So I decided to get rid of the château and its occupants. I wouldn't have thought they'd burn so well."

"You clearly don't seem to be troubled by a respect for human life, but had you no scruples about burning down a seventeenth-century château?"

"Scruples have never been my strong point."

"Indeed. Let's get back to our ending, or rather the absence of an ending. So, you claim you know nothing about the reasons why the novel is unfinished?"

"You can believe me on that point. Yes, there were any number of elegant endings I could have chosen, but none of them ever seemed suitable. I don't know, it was as if I had been expecting something else, something I've been expecting for twenty-four years, or sixty-six years, if you prefer."

"What sort of something else? For Léopoldine to be brought back to life?"

"If I knew, I wouldn't have stopped writing."

"So I was right in making a connection between the fact the novel was unfinished and your famous literary menopause."

"Of course you were right. What is there to be so proud of? When you're a journalist, all you need is a bit of skill to be right. When you're a writer, being right doesn't exist. Your profession is disgustingly easy. Whereas mine is dangerous."

"And you have managed to make it even more dangerous."

"What do you mean by this strange compliment?"

"I don't know if it's a compliment. I don't know whether it's admirable or insane, exposing yourself the way you are. Can you explain what came over you, when you decided to give a faithful narration of the story that not only was dearest to you, but also presented the greatest risk of seeing you dragged before the courts? What obscure perversion did you yield to by taking up your pen and wielding it so eloquently to provide humankind with such a blatantly transparent deed of self-incrimination?"

"But humankind doesn't give a damn! The proof of it is that for twenty-four years this novel has been collecting dust in libraries and no one, you hear me, no one has ever even talked to me about it. And that's perfectly normal because, as I told you, no one has read it."

"What about me?"

"A negligible quantity."

"What proof do you have that there aren't other negligible quantities like me around?"

"A dazzling proof: if others like you had read me—and I insist on the word 'read', in its most carnivorous sense—I would have been sent to prison long ago. You asked me a very interesting question, and the answer sticks out a mile. Here you have a murderer who has been on the loose for forty-two years.

His crimes have never been discovered, and he has become a famous writer. Far from making the most of such a comfortable situation, this sick man ventures into an absurd wager, since he has everything to lose and nothing to gain—nothing to gain, except proof of the most comical sort."

"Let me guess: he wants to prove that no one reads him."

"Better than that: he wants to prove that even the very rare people who do read him—because those people exist—have read him without reading him."

"And that's supposed to be self-evident."

"But it is, I assure you. You know, there is always a handful of idle people—vegetarians, budding critics, masochistic students, and other nosy sorts—who actually read the books they buy. I wanted to carry out my experiment on those people. I wanted to prove that I could write the worst things imaginable about my own person, with impunity: this deed of self-incrimination, as you so rightly describe it, is rigorously authentic. Yes, Mademoiselle, you have been right from beginning to end: in this book, not one detail has been made up. Of course you can find excuses for readers: no one knows a thing about my childhood, it's not the first horrible book I've written, how could anyone ever imagine I might have been so divinely handsome, and so on. But I maintain that such excuses do not hold up to scrutiny. Are you familiar with a review regarding *Hygiene and the Assassin*, one that I read in a newspaper twenty-four years ago? 'A richly symbolic fairytale, a dreamlike metaphor of original sin and, consequently, of the human condition.' When I told you that people read me without reading me! I can allow myself to stray dangerously close to the truth, and all anyone will ever see is metaphors. There's nothing surprising about that: the pseudo-reader, clad in his diving suit, can swim perfectly impermeably through my bloodiest sentences. From time to time he will exclaim with delight, 'What a lovely symbol!' That is what you call clean reading. A marvelous invention, very pleasant to practice in bed before falling asleep; it calms the mind and doesn't even dirty the sheets."

"What would you have preferred? To be read in an abattoir, or in Baghdad during a bombing?"

"Not at all, dunderhead. I'm not questioning the venue where reading takes place, but the act of reading itself. I would have preferred to be read without the frogman's suit, without a certain perspective, without a vaccination and, to be honest, without adverbs."

"You must know that reading of that nature does not exist."

"In the beginning I didn't know, but now, in the light of my brilliant proof, you can be sure I do."

"So? Shouldn't you be happy that there are as many ways of reading as there are readers?"

"You missed my point: there are no readers, and there are no ways of reading."

"Yes there are, there are readings that differ from your own, that's all. Why should your way be the only acceptable one?"

"Oh, that's enough, stop reciting your sociology textbook. Besides, I would like to know what your sociology textbook would have to say about the edifying situation I have brought to light: a writer-assassin has openly denounced himself, and not a single reader was clever enough to realize."

"I couldn't care less about the opinions of sociologists, and personally I think it's not a reader's role to act like a cop, and if no one tried to make trouble for you after this book came out, it's a good sign: it means that Fouquier-Tinville is no longer in fashion, and people are open-minded and capable of civilized reading."

"Uh-huh, I get it: you are just as rotten as all the others. I've been stupid to think you might be different from the masses."

"Well, I'm afraid you'll have to believe that I am different, however minutely, because I am the only one in my entire species who sniffed at the truth."

"Let's agree that you do have a particularly good nose. That's all. You see, you disappoint me."

"That's almost a compliment, coming from you. Am I to understand that for the space of a few minutes I was able to inspire you with a better opinion?"

"You're going to laugh: yes. You are not completely devoid of human platitudes, but you do have a very rare quality."

"I'm dying to know what it is."

"I think that it is something innate, and I'm relieved to see that your stupid apprenticeships have not managed to corrupt it."

"So what is this quality?"

"You, at least, know how to read."

Silence.

"How old are you, Mademoiselle?"

"I'm thirty."

"Twice the age of Léopoldine when she died. My poor young woman, here it is, your attenuating circumstance: you have lived far too long."

"What! You think I need an attenuating circumstance? What next!"

"You see, I'm looking for an explanation: sitting across from me is someone with a sharp mind, and who is gifted with a rare ability to read. So I've been wondering what could have spoiled such fine qualities. You have just given me the answer: time. Thirty years is far too long."

"You, at your age, are telling me this?"

"I died at the age of seventeen, Mademoiselle. And besides, for men it's not the same thing."

"Here we go."

"It's pointless trying to sound sarcastic, young lady, you know perfectly well that it's true."

"That what is true? I want to hear you say it clearly."

"It's your funeral. Well you see, men are entitled to all sorts of reprieves. Women aren't. On this last point, I am far more precise and earnest than on any other: the majority of males give females a respite of varying length before they forget about them, which is far more cowardly than killing them outright. I find this respite absurd and even disloyal toward females: because of the lapse of time, women begin to imagine that men actually need them. The truth is that from the moment they become women, the moment they leave their childhood behind, they are doomed to die. If men were gentlemen, they would kill women on the day they have their first period. But men have never been gallant, they prefer to let these unfortunate women trail their sufferings through life rather than show enough kindness to eliminate them. I know of only one male who had enough greatness, respect, love, sincerity, and courtesy to do it."

"You."

"Precisely."

The journalist threw her head back. She began to laugh, a thin, hoarse laugh. It gradually picked up speed, climbing the octaves with each new rhythm, until it became an incessant, suffocating fit. It was uncontrollable laughter, at a clinical stage.

"This makes you laugh?"

She could not reply. Her glee did not allow her the leisure of speech.

"Uncontrollable laughter: yet another female ailment. I've never seen a man double over the way women do in these cases. It must come from the uterus: everything disgusting in life comes from the uterus. Little girls do not have a uterus, I don't think, or if they do, it's a toy, a parody of a uterus. Little girls should be killed the moment their fake uterus becomes real, to spare them the type of terrific, painful hysteria you are suffering from at this very moment."

"Ah."

This "ah" was the clamor of an exhausted belly, still shaken by morbid spasms.

"Poor little thing. You've had a hard life. Who is the bastard who failed to kill you at puberty? But perhaps you didn't have a real friend at the time. Alas, I fear that Léopoldine was the only one who was that fortunate."

"Stop, I can't take it anymore."

"I understand your reaction. The belated discovery of the truth, the sudden awareness of your disappointment must come as a terrible shock . . . Your uterus is suffering a dreadful blow! Poor little female! Poor creature, spared by those cowardly males! You do have my sympathy."

"Monsieur Tach, you are the most ghastly, most entertaining individual I have ever met."

"Entertaining? I don't understand."

"I admire you. To be able to come up with a theory that is both so insane and so coherent is absolutely amazing. In the beginning I thought you were going to come out with some banal macho rubbish. But I underestimated you. Your explanation is ridiculously exaggerated and subtle at the same time: women must simply be exterminated, isn't that it?"

"Naturally. If women did not exist, things would finally start going their way."

"What an ingenious solution. Why has no one ever thought of it before?"

"In my opinion, people have thought of it, but no one before me was courageous enough to implement the solution. Because after all, the idea is there for anyone to take up. Feminism and anti-feminism are the scourge of humankind; the remedy is obvious, simple, logical: do away with women."

"Monsieur Tach: you are a genius. I admire you, and I am delighted to have met you."

"I'm going to surprise you: I too am happy to have met you."

"You're not serious."

"On the contrary. First of all, you admire me for what I am and not for what you imagined I must be: that is already a good point. And then, I know I'm going to be able to do you a huge favor, and that brings me great delight."

"What favor?"

"What do you mean, what favor? You know what it is."

"Am I to understand that you intend to do away with me, too?"

"I am beginning to think that you are worthy of such a thing, yes."

"Your praise is great, Monsieur Tach, and believe me, it affects me deeply, but . . ."

"I see that you are indeed blushing."

"But don't go to the trouble."

"Why not? I think you deserve it. You are much better than I thought at the beginning. I would like so much to help you to die."

"I am touched, but you really needn't bother; I wouldn't want you to have any problems because of me."

"Now, now, my little friend, what could I possibly risk? I only have a month and a half to live."

"I wouldn't want your posthumous reputation to be ruined on my account."

"Ruined? Why should it be ruined by such a good deed? On the contrary! People will say, 'Not even two months before he died, Prétextat Tach was still doing good deeds.' I will be an example for humankind."

"Monsieur Tach, humankind will not understand."

"Oh dear, I fear that once again you are right. But what do I care for humankind and my reputation? I would have you know, Mademoiselle, that I respect you so much that I deeply desire to do something disinterested for you alone, a good deed."

"I am sure you are greatly overestimating me."

"I don't think so."

"Open your eyes, Monsieur Tach. Didn't you say that I was

ugly, stupid, rotten, and then some? And the simple fact that I'm a woman—is that not enough to discredit me?"

"In theory, everything you say is true. But something strange is happening, Mademoiselle: theory is no longer enough. I am currently experiencing another dimension of the problem, and I am feeling delicious emotions that I had not felt for sixty-six years."

"Open your eyes, Monsieur Tach: I am not Léopoldine."

"No. And yet, you are not a stranger to her."

"She was as pretty as a picture, and you think I'm ugly."

"That's not altogether true. Your ugliness is not without beauty. There are moments when you're beautiful."

"Moments."

"There are many such moments, Mademoiselle."

"You think I'm stupid, you have no respect for me."

"Why are you so eager to discredit yourself?"

"For a very simple reason: I do not want to end up assassinated by a Nobel laureate."

A sudden chill seemed to come over the fat man.

"You would prefer a Nobel Prize for chemistry?" he asked in an icy voice.

"Very funny. I do not want to end up assassinated at all, you see, be it by a Nobel Prize winner or a grocer."

"Am I to understand that you want to put an end to your days yourself?"

"If I had wanted to commit suicide, Monsieur Tach, I would have done it long ago."

"So you say. Do you believe it's that easy?"

"I don't believe anything, it doesn't concern me. You see, I have no desire to die."

"You're not serious."

"Is it so absurd to want to live?"

"There is nothing more praiseworthy than the desire to live. But you are not living, poor silly goose! And you will never live!

Don't you understand that girls die the day they begin puberty? Worse than that, they die without disappearing. They leave life behind, not to reach the beautiful shores of death, but to begin the painful, ridiculous conjugation of a trivial, tedious verb, and they never stop conjugating it, in every tense and every mode, deconstructing it, over-constructing it, and never escaping from it."

"And what might that verb be?"

"Something like reproduce, in the rather filthy sense of the term—or ovulate, if you prefer. It is neither death, nor life, nor a state in between. There is no other name for it than being a woman: no doubt our vocabulary, with its customary insidiousness, wanted to avoid giving a name to such an abject concept."

"By what right do you claim to know what a woman's life is about?"

"A woman's non-life."

"Life or non-life, you know nothing about it."

"I would have you know, Mademoiselle, that great writers have a direct and supernatural access to the lives of others. They have no need to levitate, or to go rummaging in archives, in order to penetrate the mental universe of other individuals. All they need is a pen and a piece of paper to transfer the thoughts of others."

"Well, I never. My good man, I believe your system is a washout, if I am to judge from the inanity of your conclusions."

"Stupid woman! What would you have me believe? Or rather, what are you trying to make yourself believe? You think you're happy? There are limits to autosuggestion. Open your eyes! You're not happy, you're not alive."

"What would you know?"

"You are the one who must answer that question. How could you know whether, yes or no, you are alive, whether, yes or no, you are happy? You don't even know what happiness is.

If you had spent your childhood in an earthly paradise, like Léopoldine and myself—"

"Oh, spare me, stop making yourself out to be some exceptional case. All children are happy."

"I'm not so sure about that. No children have ever been as happy as little Léopoldine and little Prétextat. Of that I am certain."

The journalist once again threw her head back and began to laugh hysterically.

"There goes your uterus, at it again. What did I say that is so funny?"

"Please forgive me, it's those names . . . especially yours!"

"So? You have a reason to find fault with my name?"

"Find fault, no. But to be called Prétextat! I swear it's a joke. What were your parents thinking the day they decided to give you that name?"

"I forbid you to judge my parents. And frankly, I don't see what's so funny about Prétextat. It's a Christian name."

"Is it really? That makes it even funnier."

"Do not mock religion, you sacrilegious cow. I was born on February 24, which is Saint Prétextat's day; my father and mother, who were lacking in inspiration, complied with the calendar's decision."

"Heavens! Whereas if you had been born on Fat Tuesday, they would have called you Fat Tuesday, or maybe just Fat all on its own?"

"Stop blaspheming, vile creature! I would have you know, you ignoramus, that Saint Prétextat was the Archbishop of Rouen in the sixth century, and a great friend of Grégoire de Tours—who was a very fine man, you've never heard of him, naturally. It was thanks to Prétextat that the Merovingian dynasty came into being, because he was the one who married Mérovée to Brunehaut, at the risk of his own life, moreover. Which all adds up to the fact that you have no right to laugh at such an illustrious name."

"I don't see why these historical details should make your

name any less ridiculous. And as names go, your cousin's is not bad, either."

"What! How dare you make fun of my cousin's name? I forbid you! You are a monster of triviality and bad taste! Léopoldine is the most beautiful, noble, gracious, heartbreaking name that has ever been given."

"Ah."

"You heard me! I know of only one name that can even come close to Léopoldine, and that is Adèle."

"Well, well."

"Yes. Victor Hugo may have had his faults, but there is one thing that no one can ever criticize: he was a man of taste. Even when his oeuvre commits the sin of bad faith, it is beautiful and grandiose. And he gave the two most magnificent names to his two daughters. Compared to Adèle and Léopoldine, all other female first names are ghastly."

"A matter of taste."

"Not at all, imbecile! Who could care less about the taste of people like yourself—common, mediocre folk, rabble, riffraff? All that matters is the taste of people of genius, people like Victor Hugo and myself. What's more, Adèle and Léopoldine are Christian names."

"So what?"

"I see, Mademoiselle belongs to that newfangled sector of the population that likes pagan names. You would be all in favor of calling your children Krishna, Elohim, Abdallah, Chang, Empedocles, Sitting Bull, or Akhénaton, right? Grotesque. I like Christian names. In fact, what is your name?"

"Nina."

"Poor thing."

"What you mean, poor thing?"

"Yet another girl who is called neither Adèle nor Léopoldine. The world is unfair, don't you agree?"

"Have you nothing more important to say to me?"

"You find this trivial? But nothing could be more important. If your name is not Adèle or Léopoldine, that is a fundamental injustice, a primordial tragedy, above all for you, saddled with a pagan name—"

"Let me stop you right there: Nina is a Christian name. St. Nina falls on January 14, the date of your first interview."

"I do wonder what you are trying to prove with such an insignificant coincidence."

"Not as insignificant as all that. I came back from vacation on January 14, and it was on that day that I learned of your imminent demise."

"And then? Do you think that means we are connected somehow?"

"I don't think anything, but you said some extremely strange things a few minutes ago."

"Yes, I overestimated you. You have greatly disappointed me since that time. And your name—that is the ultimate debacle. Henceforth you mean nothing to me."

"I'm absolutely delighted. This way I know my life is no longer in danger."

"Your non-life, you mean. What do you plan to do with it?"

"All sorts of things: finish this interview, for example."

"How insulting. And to think that out of the goodness of my heart I could have ensured you a superb apotheosis."

"By the way, how would you have gone about killing me? It is easy, when one is an agile boy of seventeen, to murder a besotted little girl. But for an aging invalid to murder a hostile young woman—that seems like an impossible task."

"I naïvely thought you were not hostile. The fact that I am an old, obese cripple would have been no obstacle if you had loved me the way Léopoldine loved me, if you had been consenting as she was . . ."

"Monsieur Tach, you have to tell me the truth: was Léopoldine truly and consciously consenting?"

"If you had seen how docile and compliant she was, you would not ask."

"Well, it remains to be seen why she was so docile: did you drug her, or galvanize her, or lecture her, or beat her?"

"No, no, no, and no. I loved her, the way I still love her, by the way. That was more than enough. That love was of a quality that neither you nor anyone else has ever experienced. If you had known her, you would not ask me such useless questions."

"Monsieur Tach, is it impossible for you to imagine a different version of this story? You were in love, we agree on that. But that does not necessarily mean that Léopoldine wanted to die. If she went along with it, perhaps it was solely out of love for you, and not out of a desire to die."

"It's the same thing."

"It's not the same thing. Perhaps she loved you so much that she did not want to go against your wishes."

"Go against my wishes! What marvelous domestic-strife vocabulary to describe such a metaphysical moment."

"Metaphysical for you, but it might not have been for her. A moment that for you was filled with ecstasy—perhaps for her it was mere resignation."

"Look, I'm in a better position than you to be the judge of that, am I not?"

"And it's my turn to say to you that nothing could be less certain."

"What do you want, dammit! Who is the writer here, you or me?"

"You are, and that is why I find it very difficult to believe you."

"And if I were to narrate my story to you out loud, would you believe me?"

"I don't know. Go ahead and try."

"Unfortunately, it's not that easy. If I wrote about that

moment, it was because it was impossible to speak about it. Writing begins where speech leaves off, and a great mystery lies behind the passage from the unspeakable to the speakable. The written word takes over where the spoken word leaves off, and they do not overlap."

"Those are perfectly admirable ideas, Monsieur Tach, but may I remind you that we are talking about murder, not literature."

"Is there a difference?"

"The same difference that exists between the Court of Assizes and the Académie Française, I suppose."

"There is no difference between the Court of Assizes and the Académie Française."

"An interesting point, but you're getting off the topic, dear sir."

"Too true. But how can I tell the story! Do you realize I've never spoken about it in my life?"

"There's a first time for everything."

"It was August 13, 1925."

"That's already an excellent beginning."

"It was Léopoldine's birthday."

"What an amusing coincidence."

"Will you be quiet? Can't you see how this torments me, how hard it is for me to find my words?"

"I can indeed, and I'm delighted. I am relieved to know that sixty-six years later, the memory of your crime is at last tormenting you."

"You are mean-spirited and vengeful, like all females. You are right to say that *Hygiene and the Assassin* contained only two female characters: my grandmother and my aunt. Léopoldine was not a female character, she was—and will be, forever—a child, a miraculous being, beyond the sexes."

"But not beyond sex, if I am to believe what I've read in your book."

"We alone knew that it is not necessary to be pubescent to make love; on the contrary: puberty comes and spoils everything. It diminishes sensuality and the capacity for ecstasy and abandonment. No one makes love as well as a child does."

"So when you said you were a virgin, you were lying."

"No, I wasn't. In common parlance, males cannot lose their virginity until after puberty. Whereas I never made love after puberty."

"I see that you are playing with words, yet again."

"Not at all, you simply know nothing about it. But I would appreciate it if you would stop interrupting me all the time."

"You interrupted a life; allow others to interrupt your logorrhea."

"Come now, my logorrhea suits you fine. It makes your job so much easier."

"I suppose that's true. Well then, train your logorrhea on August 13, 1925."

"August 13, 1925: the most beautiful day ever. I hope that every human being, at least once in their life, will have an August 13, 1925—because it is more than a mere date. That day was a consecration. The most beautiful day of the most beautiful summer, balmy and breezy, the air light beneath the dense trees. Léopoldine and I had begun our day at around one o'clock in the morning, after our ritual sleep of roughly an hour and a half. You might think that with such a timetable we were continuously exhausted: that was never the case. We were so avid for our Eden that we often had difficulty falling asleep. It was only at the age of eighteen, after the fire at the château, that I began to sleep eight hours a day: people who are too happy or unhappy are incapable of such long absences. Léopoldine and I liked nothing better than to wake up. In the summer, it was even better, because we spent the night outside and slept in the heart of the forest, wrapped in a pearl damask bedspread that I had stolen from the château. Whoever woke up first would contemplate the other, and a gaze was enough to rouse us. On August 13, 1925, I was the first to wake, at around one o'clock, and she joined me shortly after that. We had all the time in the world to do everything a beautiful night invites one to do, everything which, on a damask bedspread that was less and less of pearl and more and more of dead leaves, could elevate us to the dignity of the hierophant—I liked to call Léopoldine the *hierinfanta*, I was already so cultured, so spiritual, but I'm getting off the subject—"

"Indeed."

"On August 13, 1925, as I was saying. An absolutely calm, dark night, unusually gentle. It was Léopoldine's birthday, but that meant nothing to us: for the last three years, time had no longer mattered. We had not changed so much as an atom; we had simply grown in length, prodigiously, but in no way had this amusing stretching of our bodies altered our shapeless, hairless, odorless, infantile constitution. So I did not wish her a happy birthday that morning. I believe I did something much better, I gave a lesson in summer to summer itself. It was the last time in my life that I made love. I did not know that, but no doubt the forest knew it, because it was as silent as an old voyeur. It was when the sun rose above the hills that the wind began to blow, banishing the nocturnal clouds to reveal a sky almost as pure as we were."

"What admirable lyricism."

"Stop interrupting me. Let's see, where was I?"

"August 13, 1925, sunrise, post-coital."

"Thank you, Mademoiselle the clerk of the court."

"You're welcome, Monsieur the murderer."

"I prefer my title to yours."

"I prefer my title to Léopoldine's."

"If you had seen her that morning! She was the most beautiful creature in the world, an immense smooth and white *infanta* with dark hair and dark eyes. In the summer, with the exception of the very rare times we went to the château, we lived naked—the estate was so vast that we never ran into anyone. So we would spend most of our days in the lakes, to which I attributed amniotic virtues, which may not have been as absurd as it seems, given the results. But the cause hardly matters; all that mattered was this miracle that occurred daily— a miracle of time frozen for eternity, or at least that is what we believed. And on August 13, 1925, we had every reason to believe as much, as we gazed upon each other in a stupor. That morning, like any other, I dove into the lake without hesitating, and I laughed at Léopoldine, because she always took forever to get into the icy water. My mockery was yet another pleasant ritual, because my cousin was never more lovely to behold than when she stood with one foot in the lake, pale and laughing from the cold, swearing to me that she would never manage, then gradually unfolding her long pale limbs to join me, as if in slow motion, like some shivering wading bird, her lips blue, her big eyes full of terror—fright became her—stammering that it was awful—"

"You are horribly sadistic!"

"What would you know! If you had the slightest knowledge of pleasure, you would know that fear and pain and above all shivers make the best preludes. Once she was all the way in the water, like me, the cold gave way to fluidity, to the gentle ease of life in the water. That morning, like every morning that summer, we marinated endlessly, sometimes gliding together toward the depths of the lake, our eyes open, looking at our bodies that were green in the glistening water, sometimes swimming on the surface, competing for speed, sometimes bobbing in place, clinging to the branches of the weeping willows, speaking the way children speak, but with a greater knowledge of childhood, sometimes floating for hours, drinking up the sky with our eyes, in the perfect silence of icy waters. When the cold had completely penetrated us, we pulled ourselves out onto huge slabs of stone to dry in the sun. The wind on that August 13 was particularly pleasant and quickly warmed us. Léopoldine dove in again first, and held on to the little island where I was still getting warm. It was her turn to make fun of me. I can see her as if it were only yesterday, her elbows on the stone and her chin on her crossed wrists, her impertinent expression and her long hair which, in the water, undulated to the rhythm of her scarcely visible legs, almost frightening in their faraway whiteness. We were so happy, so unreal, so in love, so beautiful, all for the last time."

"No elegies, please. If it was the last time, that was your fault."

"So? Does that make things any less sad?"

"On the contrary, it merely makes them sadder, but because you were responsible, you have no right to complain."

"No right? The last thing I want to hear. I don't give a damn about rights, and however responsible I might have been in the matter, I think I do have a reason to complain. Besides, my responsibility in the matter was negligible."

"Oh, really? Maybe it was the wind that strangled her?"

"It was I, but it was not my fault."

"You mean you strangled her in a moment of distraction?"

"No, silly woman, I mean it was the fault of nature, life, hormones, and all that rubbish. Let me tell you my story and allow me to be elegiac. I was describing Léopoldine's white legs— such a mysterious whiteness, particularly when seen through the green darkness of the water. To stay afloat horizontally, my cousin was slowly kicking her long legs, I could see each one rising alternately to the surface—no sooner did one foot have time to emerge than her leg was already on its way down, swallowed by the void to make way for the whiteness of the other leg, and so on. On that August 13, 1925, lying on my stony island, I could not get enough of that graceful spectacle. I don't know how long the moment lasted. It was interrupted by an abnormal detail, of a crudeness I still find shocking: the ballet of Léopoldine's legs caused something to rise up from the depths of the lake, a thin stream of red fluid, of a very special density, judging from its reluctance to mingle with pure water."

"In short, it was blood."

"How crude you are."

"Your cousin, quite simply, had gotten her period for the first time."

"You're disgusting."

"There's nothing disgusting about it, it's normal."

"Precisely."

"This attitude isn't like you, Monsieur Tach. You are such an outspoken enemy of bad faith, the carnivorous defendant of coarse language, and now here you act offended, like some hero out of Oscar Wilde, because you've heard someone call a spade a spade. You may have been madly in love, but your love could not displace Léopoldine from the human race."

"Yes it could."

"This can't be true: is this you, the sarcastic genius, with your Célinian way with words, the cynical vivisectionist, the metaphysician of ridicule, producing drivel worthy of a baroque adolescent?"

"Shut up, iconoclast. It's not drivel."

"Isn't it? A love story between two little aristocrats, the young boy in love with his noble cousin, the romantic wager against time, the limpid lakes in the legendary forest—if that's not drivel, then nothing here on earth is."

"If you would allow me to tell you the rest, you would understand that it really is not a driveling story."

"Then go ahead, try and convince me. It won't be easy, because what you've told me so far has filled me with dismay. And this boy who is incapable of accepting the fact his cousin has her first period—it's grotesque. It stinks of vegetarian lyricism."

"What comes next is not vegetarian, but I do need a minimum of silence to be able to narrate it."

"I promise nothing; it's difficult to listen to you without reacting."

"Wait at least until I have finished before you react. Shit, where was I? You've made me lose the thread."

"Blood in the water."

"Heavens above, that's right. Imagine my shock: the jarring intrusion of that red, hot color amidst so much paleness—the icy water, the chlorotic darkness of the lake, the whiteness of Léopoldine's shoulders, her lips as blue as mercury sulfate, and then above all her legs, like imperceptible epiphanies evoking, in their unfathomable slowness, some sort of Hyperborean caress. No, it was unacceptable: the source of such repulsive effusion could not lie between those legs."

"Repulsive!"

"Repulsive, I insist. Repulsive because of what it was, and even more so because of what it signified—a terrible rite, a passage from mythical life to hormonal life, a passage from eternal life to cyclical life. You have to be a vegetarian to be content with cyclical eternity. In my opinion, it's a contradiction in terms. For Léopoldine and me, eternity could not be conceived in any other way than in the first person of a singular singular, because it encompassed both of us. Cyclical eternity, on the other hand, suggests that a third party will come and interfere with other people's lives—and one is supposed to go along with this expropriation, to be happy about this whole usurpatory process! I have nothing but scorn for those who accept such a sinister comedy: I scorn them not so much for their sheep-like capacities of resignation as for the anemia of their love. Because if they were capable of true love, they would not submit so spinelessly, they could not bear to witness the suffering of those whom they claim to love, and without any selfish cowardice they would take responsibility for sparing their loved ones from such an abject fate. That stream of blood in the lake water signified the end of eternity for Léopoldine. And because I loved her deeply, I decided to restore her to that eternity, without further ado."

"I am beginning to understand."

"You took long enough."

"I'm beginning to understand how very sick you really are."

"Well, what will you have to say about what's next, then?"

"With you, I can always be sure of the worst."

"With me or without me, you may always be sure of the worst, but I believe I have spared at least one person from the worst. Léopoldine saw my gaze stop abruptly behind her and she turned around. She got out of the water as quickly as she could, as if she were terrified. She hoisted herself up next to me onto the stony island. There was no longer any doubt as to the origin of the stream of blood. My cousin was filled with aversion, which I could well understand. All through the three preceding years, we had never evoked this possibility. We had a sort of tacit agreement regarding the behavior we would adopt in this event—an event that was so unacceptable that in order to preserve our blissful stupor, we preferred to keep to a tacit agreement."

"This is what I was afraid of. Léopoldine had asked nothing of you, and you killed her in the name of a 'tacit agreement' that stemmed from the unhealthy darkness of your imagination alone."

"She did not ask me anything explicitly, but it wasn't necessary."

"Just as I said. In a few minutes you're going to start bragging about the virtue of what remains unsaid."

"Someone like you would have wanted a contract drawn up and signed in the presence of a lawyer, is that it?"

"I would have preferred anything to the way you behaved."

"It hardly matters what you would have preferred. The only thing that mattered was Léopoldine's salvation."

"The only thing that mattered was your conception of Léopoldine's salvation."

"It was also her conception. The proof, dear Mademoiselle, is that we said nothing to each other. I kissed her eyes very softly and she understood. She seemed calm, and she smiled. It all happened very quickly. Three minutes later she was dead."

"What, just like that, without any time elapsing at all? That's . . . that's monstrous."

"You would have wanted it to last for two hours, like at the opera?"

"But you don't just go around killing people that way."

"Oh, no? I wasn't aware that there are was a prescribed way of doing it. Is there a treatise on etiquette for assassins? A handbook on *savoir-vivre* for victims? Next time, I promise you that I will kill more courteously."

"Next time? Thank God, there will not be a next time. In the meantime, you make me want to vomit."

"In the meantime? You intrigue me."

"So, you claimed to love her, and you strangled her without even telling her one last time?"

"She knew it. My gesture was the proof, after all. If I had not loved her so deeply, I would not have killed her."

"How can you be sure that she knew?"

"We never talked about such things, we were on the same wavelength. And besides, we weren't talkative. But let me tell you about the strangling. I've never had the opportunity to talk about it, but I like thinking about it—how many times have I relived that beautiful scene in the private realm of my memory?"

"What a way to pass the time!"

"You'll see, you'll begin to like it, too."

"Like what? Your memories, or strangling?"

"Love. But let me tell you the story, please."

"Since you insist."

"There we were on the stony island, in the middle of the

lake. From the moment that death was decreed, Eden, which had just been brutally wrenched from us two minutes earlier, was restored to us for three. We were absolutely aware that all we had left was one hundred and eighty seconds of Eden, so we were determined to do things properly, and we did them properly. Oh, I know what you're thinking: that all the credit for a good job of strangling belongs to the strangler alone. That is not true. The victim is far less passive than you would think. Have you seen that very bad film made by a barbarian—a Japanese filmmaker, if my memory serves me correctly—which ends with a scene of strangling that lasts roughly thirty-two minutes?"

"Yes, Oshima's *In the Realm of the Senses.*"

"The strangling scene is botched. As something of an expert, I can assure you that it doesn't happen like that. First of all, a strangling that lasts thirty-two minutes: I ask you, such bad taste! It's as if there were a reluctance on the part of all art forms to accept that murders are alert, rapid events. Hitchcock at least had figured that much out. And then, another thing that this Japanese gentleman did not understand: there is nothing languid or painful about strangling; on the contrary, it's invigorating, it's fresh."

"Fresh? Not the way I'd describe it! Why not say nourishing, while you're at it?"

"Why not, indeed? You do feel revitalized, when you've strangled someone you love."

"The way you talk about it, you'd think you do it on a regular basis."

"All it takes is to have done something once—but done it deeply—in order to do it again continually, throughout your entire life. To this end, it is imperative that the crucial scene be one of aesthetic perfection. That Japanese man must not have known this, or else he was extremely clumsy, because his strangling scene is ugly, even ridiculous: the woman who is strangling looks as if she's pumping, and the victim looks as if he's being crushed under a steamroller. My own strangling scene, on the other hand, and you can take my word for it, was splendid."

"I don't doubt it. And yet I would like to ask you one question: why did you choose strangling? Given where you were, drowning would have been more logical. That was, moreover, the explanation you gave your cousin's parents, when you brought them the corpse—hardly a believable explanation, given the marks on her neck. So, why didn't you simply drown the child?"

"An excellent question. It did cross my mind on that day of August 13, 1925. I reached my decision very quickly. I told myself that if all Léopoldines were to die by drowning, it would become something of a standard procedure, subject to the law of genre, and that would be altogether too trite. Not to mention the fact that the memory of Victor Hugo might have been outraged by such servile plagiarism."[1]

"So you renounced the idea of drowning to avoid creating a reference. But the choice of strangling exposed you to other references."

"True, yet I did not really take that into consideration. No, my decision to strangle my cousin was based, above all, upon the beauty of her neck. Whether you looked at her nape or at her throat, she had a sublime neck, long and supple, admirably conceived. Such finesse! To strangle someone like me, you would need at least two pairs of hands. With a delicate neck like hers, it was incredibly easy to put my hands around her."

"And if she had not had this beautiful neck, would you have not strangled her?"

"I don't know. I might have done it all the same, because I'm a very hands-on sort of person. And as far as death techniques go, you can't get much more hands-on than strangling. It gives your hands an incomparable impression of sensual plenitude."

---

[1] Victor Hugo's eldest daughter Léopoldine died at the age of 19 in a boating accident. (T.N.)

"So you see, you did do it for your own pleasure! Why are you trying to sell me on the idea that you strangled her for her own salvation?"

"My dear young woman, you have the excuse that you know nothing about theology. However, since you claim to have read all my books, you ought to understand. I wrote a fine novel entitled *Concomitant Grace*, which describes the ecstasy that God gives us in the course of our actions to make them meritorious. I did not invent the notion, it's one that true mystics know well. You see, as I was strangling Léopoldine, my pleasure was a grace concomitant with the salvation of my beloved."

"You're going to end up telling me that *Hygiene and the Assassin* is a Catholic novel."

"No. It's an edifying novel."

"So please complete my edification, and tell me the last scene."

"I'm getting there. Everything happened with the simplicity of a masterpiece. Léopoldine sat on my lap, facing me. Please note, Mademoiselle the clerk of the court, that she did so on her own initiative."

"That doesn't prove a thing."

"Do you think she was surprised, when I put my hands around her neck, and when I began to tighten the vise? Not at all. We were smiling to each other, gazing into each other's eyes. This was not a parting, because we were dying together. The pronoun 'I' meant both of us."

"How romantic."

"Don't you agree? You will never be able to imagine how beautiful Léopoldine was, particularly at that moment. One mustn't strangle someone whose neck is scrunched down between their shoulders, it's not aesthetically pleasing. However, strangling is very fitting for long, graceful necks."

"Your cousin must have made a most elegant strangling victim."

"Ravishingly elegant. Between my hands I could feel her delicate cartilage gradually giving way."

"He who kills by the cartilage shall die by the cartilage."

The fat man looked at the journalist, stunned.

"Did you hear what you said?"

"I said it deliberately."

"That's extraordinary! You are a clairvoyant. Why did I not think of this myself? We already knew that Elzenveiverplatz Syndrome was the cancer of murderers, but we were lacking an explanation: now we have it! Those ten convicts in Cayenne must have had a go at their victims' cartilage. Our Lord said as much: the arms of murderers always turn against them. Thanks to you, Mademoiselle, I know at last why I have cartilage cancer! Didn't I tell you that theology was the science of sciences!"

The novelist seemed to have attained the intellectual ecstasy of the scholar who after twenty years of research finally discovers the coherence of his system. His gaze was deconstructing some invisible absolute, while his greasy forehead pearled with moisture like a mucous membrane.

"I am still waiting for the end of the story, Monsieur Tach."

The slim young woman contemplated the fat old man's illuminated features with disgust.

"The end of the story, Mademoiselle? The story doesn't end, it's only just beginning! And you are the one who has just made me understand it. The purpose of cartilage is to assist articulation. Articulation of the body, but also of this story!"

"What are you jabbering on about now ?"

"You may think I'm jabbering, but it's the jabbering of coherence regained! Thanks to you, Mademoiselle, I shall at last be able to continue and perhaps even finish my novel. Underneath *Hygiene and the Assassin*, I will place a subtitle: 'A Story of Cartilage.' The finest testament in the world, don't you think? But I shall have to hurry, I have so little time left to write! My God, such urgency! What an ultimatum!"

"Whatever you like, but before you go on to write the rest of the story, you have to tell me the end of what happened on August 13, 1925."

"I won't prolong it, I'll make it a flashback! Here's what I mean: cartilage is the missing link, the ambivalent articulation that allows me to go from the past to the future, but also from the future to the past, to have access to all time, to eternity! You are asking me for the end of August 13, 1925? But there is no end to August 13, 1925, because eternity began on that day. So, today, you may think that it is January 18, 1991, you may think that it's winter, and that we are at war in the Persian Gulf. A vulgar error! The calendar stopped sixty-five and a half years ago! It's the middle of summer, and I am a beautiful child."

"Not that I can see."

"Because you're not looking at me intensely enough. Look at my hands: they are so pretty, so fine."

"They are, I must admit. You may be obese and shapeless, but you have kept graceful hands, a page boy's hands."

"You see? It's a sign, naturally: my hands have played an enormous part in this story. Ever since August 13, 1925, my hands have never ceased from strangling. Can't you see that right now, as I am speaking to you, I am in the process of strangling Léopoldine?"

"No."

"But I am. Look at my hands. See my knuckles curling round that swanlike neck, look at my fingers massaging her cartilage, sinking into the spongy tissue, the spongy tissue that will become text."

"Monsieur Tach, I have caught you red-handed using a metaphor."

"It's not a metaphor. What is text, if not gigantic verbal cartilage?"

"Whether you like it or not, it's a metaphor."

"If you could just see things as a whole, the way I see them at the moment, you would understand. Metaphors were invented to enable human beings to establish a coherence between the fragments in their vision. When this fragmentation disappears, metaphors no longer have any purpose. Poor little blind girl! Someday perhaps you will be able to see things as a whole, and your eyes will open, as mine have finally opened, after sixty-five and a half years of blindness."

"Don't you think you need a tranquilizer, Monsieur Tach? You seem to me to be dangerously overexcited."

"With good reason. I had forgotten one could be this happy."

"What reason do you have to be happy?"

"I told you: I am in the process of strangling Léopoldine."

"And this makes you happy?"

"Indeed it does! My cousin is approaching seventh heaven. She has her head thrown back, her ravishing mouth is half open, her huge eyes are swallowing infinity, unless it's the other way round, her face is one big smile, and there we are, she's dead. I loosen my embrace, I let her body slip into the lake, and it floats—Léopoldine's eyes gaze skyward in ecstasy, then she sinks and disappears."

"Aren't you going to fish her out?"

"Not right away. First of all I have to think about what I've just done."

"Are you pleased with yourself?"

"Yes. I burst out laughing."

"You're laughing?"

"Yes. I am thinking about how, normally, assassins draw their victim's blood, whereas I, without spilling a single drop of her blood, have killed her to put an end to her hemorrhage, to restore her to her original, unbloodied immortality. The paradox of it makes me laugh."

"Your sense of humor is extraordinarily inappropriate."

"And then I look at the lake: the wind has ruffled the surface evenly, erasing even the last traces of Léopoldine's fall. And I think it makes a worthy shroud for my cousin. I suddenly call to mind the drowning of Hugo's daughter in Villequier and recall my motto: 'Careful, Prétextat, no law of genre, no plagiarism.' And so I dive into the water, far into the greenish depths where my cousin is waiting for me, still so close, yet already enigmatic, like a submerged vestige. Her long hair is floating high above her face, and to me she has the mysterious smile of Atlantis."

A long silence.

"And then?"

"Oh, after that . . . I lift her back up to the surface and take her light, supple body in my arms, like seaweed. I carry her back to the château, where the arrival of these two charming naked bodies makes a great impression. They quickly discover that Léopoldine is far more naked than I am. What could be more naked than a corpse? Then there begin all those ridiculous effusions of emotion—cries, tears, lamentation, imprecations against destiny and my negligence, despair—a scene of such kitsch, worthy of a third-rate scribbler: the moment I am no longer in charge of arranging things, these scenes begin to display the most hideous bad taste."

"You might try and understand their distress, particularly that of the victim's parents."

"Distress, distress . . . that seems quite exaggerated to me. To them Léopoldine was never anything but a charming decorative idea. They almost never saw her. For almost three years we had been residing in the forest, and they never worried about where we were. You know, those lords and ladies live in a world of fairly conventional imagery; in this instance, they understood that the theme of the scene was 'The Corpse of the Drowned Child Restored to Its Parents.' You may imagine the naïvely Shakespearean and Hugolian references that prevailed in the minds of those good people. They were not weeping for

Léopoldine de Planèze de Saint-Sulpice, but for Léopoldine Hugo, for Ophelia, for all the drowned innocence in the world. For them, the *hierinfanta* was an abstract corpse, one might even say she was a purely cultural phenomenon, and their lamentations merely served to prove the profound literacy of their sensibilities. No, the only person who knew the real Léopoldine, the only person who might have a concrete reason to weep over her death, was me."

"But you weren't weeping."

"On the part of an assassin, to weep for one's victim would betray a blatant lack of single-mindedness. Besides, I was in a good position to know that my cousin was happy, and would be happy forever after. So I was serene and smiling in the midst of all their shaggy lamentations."

"Something you were subsequently reproached for, I suppose."

"You suppose correctly."

"I will have to make do with these suppositions, given the fact your novel does not go much further."

"Indeed. You will have noticed that *Hygiene and the Assassin* is a very aquatic work. To end this book with the fire in the château would have ruined its perfect liquid coherence. There's nothing more annoying than artists who couple water with fire: such banal dualism is downright pathological."

"Don't try and fool me—it is hardly metaphysical consider-ations of the sort that convinced you to abandon your narration so abruptly. You said as much yourself, earlier on: some myste-rious cause blocked your writing. Let me recapitulate the final pages: you leave Léopoldine's corpse in the arms of her weeping parents, after providing them with an explanation so brief that it was downright cynical. The last sentence in the novel reads as follows: 'And I went up to my room.'"

"Not a bad ending."

"That's as may be, but you will agree the reader might be hungry for more."

"Well, there's nothing wrong with that."

"For a metaphorical reading, yes. Not for the type of flesh-eating reading that you recommend."

"Dear Mademoiselle, you are both right and wrong. You are right, in that something mysterious forced me to leave this novel unfinished. And nevertheless you are wrong because, like any good journalist, you want me to continue my narration in a linear fashion. Believe me, that would have been sordid, because what followed on August 13 was never, to this very day, anything more than a disgusting, grotesque decline. From 14 August on, the thin, sober child that I had been turned into a terrible glutton. Was it the void left by Léopoldine's death? I continuously craved the most revolting food—a taste which I have preserved. In six months, my weight tripled, I became pubescent and horrible, I lost all my hair, I lost everything. I told you about my family's conventional imagery: this imagery required that when a loved one died, the family should fast and lose weight. Therefore, everyone at the château was fasting and losing weight, whereas I, all alone of my scandalous species, stuffed my face and blew up like a balloon before their very eyes. I recall, not without a certain mirth, the contrast between our meals: my grandparents, my uncle, and my aunt hardly smudged their plates, and they watched with consternation as I emptied out the dishes and gobbled everything down like a swine. My bulimia and the suspicious bruises they had seen on Léopoldine's neck fuelled their conclusions. No one spoke to me anymore, and it was as if I were in a halo of hateful suspicion."

"Well-founded suspicion."

"You must realize that I wanted to destroy an atmosphere that was gradually ceasing to amuse me. And you must imagine that I would have found it abhorrent to demystify my splendid novel with such a lamentable epilogue. So you were mistaken to want the novel to continue in due form, and yet you were right to think that the story deserved a real ending—but I could not possibly know that ending before today, since you are the one who has brought it to me."

"I brought you an ending for your novel?"

"It is what you are doing at this very moment."

"If you are trying to make me feel ill at ease, well, you've succeeded, but I would like an explanation."

"You already provided a supremely interesting closing element, with your comment about cartilage."

"I hope you don't intend to spoil that fine novel by grafting onto it the cartilaginous nonsense you flung at me just now."

"Why not? It's an absolutely great find."

"I would be angry with myself for suggesting such a bad ending. You would do better to leave your novel unfinished."

"I'll be the judge of that. But there's something else you're going to bring me."

"And what is that?"

"You yourself will show me, my dear child. Let's move on to the climax, shall we? We have waited the prescribed amount of time."

"What climax?"

"Don't act all innocent. Aren't you going to tell me who you are, in the end? What mysterious ties you might have with me?"

"No ties whatsoever."

"Are you not the last survivor of the Planèze de Saint-Sulpice lineage?"

"You know very well that the family died without progeny—you had something to do with it, after all."

"Might you be a distant relation of the Tach family?"

"You know perfectly well that you are the last descendent of the Tach dynasty."

"Are you the tutor's granddaughter?"

"Absolutely not! What will you dream up next?"

"Who was your ancestor, then? The steward or the butler of the château? The gardener? A chambermaid? The cook?"

"Stop right there, Monsieur Tach; I have no connection of any sort with your family, your château, your village, or your past."

"That's unacceptable."

"Why?"

"You would not have gone to so much trouble in your research if you did not have some obscure connection with me."

"I have caught you *flagrante delicto* under the influence of your profession, monsieur. Like any self-respecting obsessive writer, you cannot stand the thought that there is no mysterious correlation between your characters. Genuine novelists are basically genealogists at heart. I'm sorry to disappoint you: I am a stranger to you."

"I am sure you are wrong. Perhaps you do not even know yourself what family, historical, geographical, or genetic tie unites us, but there can be no doubt, such a tie must exist. Let's see . . . perhaps one of your ancestors died of drowning? Were there any stranglings in your immediate entourage?"

"Stop raving, Monsieur Tach. Your search for similarities between our two cases is in vain—and what meaning might any such similarities hold? What does seem significant is your need to establish a similarity."

"Significant in what respect?"

"That is the true question, and you yourself will have to answer."

"I see, once again I have to do everything myself. Basically, the theoreticians of the *nouveau roman* were inveterate pranksters: the truth is that there is nothing new under the sun. Faced with a shapeless, senseless universe, a writer is obliged to play the demiurge. Without the remarkable assistance of his pen, the world would never have been able to give shape to things, and the stories of men would always have been wide open, like some horrible madhouse. And here you are, in keeping with this multi-millennial tradition, begging me to play the glassblower, to make up your own text, and punctuate your dialogue."

"Well go ahead then, blow."

"I have been doing little else, my child. Can't you see that I too am begging you? Help me to give meaning to this story, and do not have the bad faith to tell me that we have no need of meaning: we need meaning more than anything else. Don't you realize! For sixty-six years, I have been waiting to meet someone like you—so don't go trying to make me believe you're just any-body. You cannot deny that a strange denominator must have orchestrated an interview like this. Let me put the question to you one last time—I repeat, one last time, because patience is not my strong point—and I implore you, tell me the truth: who are you?"

"Alas, Monsieur Tach."

"What do you mean, alas? Have you nothing else to say?"

"I do, but can you bear to hear my response?"

"I would prefer the worst possible response to an absence of response."

"Precisely. My response is an absence of response."

"Be clear, if you please."

"You asked who I am. Well, you already know, not because I told you, but because you already said so yourself. Have you already forgotten? Earlier, amidst your hail of insults, you were spot on."

"Go ahead, I am perplexed."

"Monsieur Tach, I am a filthy little muckraker. There is nothing else to be said, you can believe me on that score. I am truly sorry. You may be sure that I would have loved to have another response for you, but you demanded the truth and that is my only truth."

"I will never believe that."

"You are wrong. On the subject of my life and my genealogy, I can tell you no more than very ordinary things. If I had not been a journalist, I would never have tried to meet you. You may search all you like, you will always come to the same con-clusion: I am a filthy little muckraker."

"I do not know if you fully realize what a response like this suggests in the way of horrors."

"Indeed, I do not realize."

"No, you do not realize, or not well enough. Let me describe those horrors to you: imagine an old man who is dying, absolutely alone and without hope. Imagine that a young person comes to see him, after he has waited sixty-six years, and suddenly she restores hope to the old man by bringing his buried past back to life. There are two possibilities: either this person is a mysterious archangel who is close to the old man, and it's an apotheosis; or this person is a perfect stranger motivated by the most unhealthy curiosity, and in that case, allow me to contend that it is sordid: it is grave-digging coupled with an abuse of trust, it is stealing from a dying man his most precious treasure by holding up before him the promise of some miraculous retribution and, in the end, giving him nothing in exchange but a huge pile of shit. When you arrived here, you found an old man dying amidst his beautiful memories, resigned to the fact he no longer has a present. When you leave here, you will leave behind an old man dying in the rotting decomposition of his memories, and desperate that he no longer has a present. If you had a bit of heart or human decency, you would have lied to me, you would have invented a tie between us. Now it's too late, so if you do have a scrap of humane decency, finish me off, put an end to my disgust, because it's causing me unbearable suffering."

"You're exaggerating. I do not believe I misrepresented your memories to that degree."

"My novel needs an ending. Through your maneuvers, you made me believe that you were bringing me that ending. I had no longer dared to hope, I was coming back to life after an interminable hibernation—and then, shamelessly, you show me that your hands are empty, you have brought me nothing but the illusion of a sudden new plot twist. At my age, one can no longer bear such things. Were it not for you, I would have died leaving an unfinished novel behind. Because of you, my very death will be unfinished."

"Have you finished with your stylistic arabesques?"

"Arabesques indeed! Might you have forgotten that you have dispossessed me of my substance? I'm going to teach you something, Mademoiselle: I am not the assassin, you are!"

"Pardon?"

"You heard me. You are the assassin, and you have killed two people. As long as Léopoldine was still alive in my memory, her death was an abstraction. But you have killed her memory with your muckraking intrusion, and by killing that memory, you have killed what remained of me."

"Sophistry."

"You would know that it is not sophistry, if you had the vaguest knowledge of love. But how could a filthy little muck-raker understand what love is? I have never met a greater stranger to love."

"If love is what you say it is, I'm relieved to be a stranger to it."

"Clearly, I have taught you nothing."

"I really wonder what you could have taught me, other than how to strangle people."

"I would have liked to teach you that in strangling Léopol-dine, I saved her from the only true death, which is to be for-gotten. You may think of me as an assassin, when in fact I am one of the rare human beings who has killed no one. Look around you and look at yourself: the world is swarming with assassins, that is, people who allow themselves to forget those they claimed to love. To forget someone: have you really thought about what that means? Forgetfulness is a gigantic ocean where only one ship sails, the ship of memory. For the vast majority of human beings, that ship is no more than a miserable tub which takes on water at the slightest opportunity, and whose captain, an unscrupulous character, is only interested in saving money. Do you know what that foul expression implies? A daily sacrifice, among the crew, of those who are deemed superfluous. And do you know which ones are deemed superfluous? Do you think it's the bastards, the bores, the idiots? Not at all: the ones who get thrown overboard are the useless ones—those who have already been used. The ones who have already given the best of themselves, so what do they have left to give? Come now, no pity, let's clean ship, and hup! over the railing they go, and the ocean swallows them, implacably. There you have it, dear Mademoiselle, this is how the most ordinary of assassinations is carried out, in all impunity. I have never subscribed to that dreadful slaughter, and you stand here today accusing me in the name of my innocence, in accordance with what human beings like to call justice and which is in fact a sort of instruction manual for informing on others."

"Who said anything about informing? I have no intention of denouncing you."

"Really? Well then, you are even worse than I imagined. As a rule, muckrakers have the decency to come up with a cause. But you stir up shit gratuitously, for the sole pleasure of stinking up the atmosphere. When you leave here you will rub your hands together, knowing for sure that you have not wasted your day, since you have smeared dirt across someone else's world. You have chosen a fine profession, Mademoiselle."

"If I understand correctly, you would rather I dragged you before the courts?"

"Of course. Have you thought for a moment of my agony, if you do not denounce me, if you leave me alone and empty in this apartment after what you have done to me? Whereas at least if you drag me before the court, it will entertain me."

"Sorry, Monsieur Tach, you'll have to turn yourself in: I won't stoop to that sort of thing."

"Yes, you're above all that, aren't you? You belong to the worst sort of people, those who would rather pollute than destroy. Can you explain to me what was going through your head the day you decided to come and torture me? To what gratuitously foul instinct did you succumb that day?"

"You've known that from the beginning, monsieur: have you forgotten our wager? I wanted to see you crawl at my feet. Now with everything you've told me, I want it more than ever. So go ahead and crawl, since you've lost our wager."

"I may indeed have lost, but I prefer my lot to yours."

"Good for you. Crawl."

"Is it your female vanity that wants to see me crawl?"

"It is my desire for revenge. Crawl."

"So you have not understood a thing."

"My criteria will never be yours, and I've understood perfectly well. I hold life to be the most precious blessing, and none of your words will change any of that. If it weren't for you, Léopoldine would have lived, with everything horrible that may imply, but also everything beautiful. There is nothing more to say. Crawl."

"After all, I'm not holding it against you."

"That's all I need. Crawl."

"You live in a sphere that is completely foreign to me. It's normal for you not to understand."

"Your condescension is touching. Crawl."

"In fact, I'm far more tolerant than you are: I am capable of accepting the fact that you live with other criteria. But you aren't. For you, there is only one way of seeing things. You are narrow-minded."

"Monsieur Tach, you may be sure that your existential considerations do not interest me. I am ordering you to crawl, and that's it."

"So be it. But how do you expect me to crawl? Have you forgotten that I'm a cripple?"

"That's true. Let me help you."

The journalist stood up, lifted the fat man from under his arms, and with a great effort managed to heave him onto the carpet, face down.

"Help! Help!"

But in that position, the novelist's lovely voice was muffled, and no one could hear him, except the young woman.

"Crawl."

"I cannot bear to be on my stomach! My doctor won't allow it."

"Crawl."

"Shit! I'm about to suffocate, any minute now!"

"So then you'll know what suffocation is, since you inflicted it on a little girl. Crawl."

"It was for her salvation."

"Well then, it is for your salvation that I'm exposing you to the risk of suffocation. You are a despicable old man whom I want to save from decline. So it's the same thing. Crawl."

"But I've already declined! I've done nothing but decline for sixty-five and a half years!"

"In that case, I want to see you decline some more. Go on, decline."

"You can't say that, there is no such thing as an imperative of the verb 'to decline.'"

"I really couldn't care less. But if the verb 'decline' bothers you with its lack of imperative, I know another one that will work very well: crawl."

"This is terrible, I'm suffocating, I'm going to die!"

"Well, well. I thought you looked on death as a good thing."

"And it is, but I don't want to die right away."

"No? Why delay such a happy event?"

"Because I've just realized something, and I want to tell you before I die.

"All right. I will agree to turn you over onto your back, but on one condition: first of all you have to crawl at my feet."

"I promise you I'll try."

"I'm not asking you to try, I'm ordering you to crawl. If you don't manage, I'll let you die."

"All right, I'll crawl."

And the huge sweaty mass dragged itself along six feet of carpet, puffing like a locomotive.

"This is positively orgasmic for you, I suppose?"

"It is indeed. All the more so knowing that I'm avenging someone. I have the impression that if I look through your hypertrophied body I can see a slim silhouette which, through your suffering, is finding relief."

"Theatrical and ridiculous."

"You don't like it? Do you want to crawl some more?"

"I swear to you, it's time to turn me over. I can feel my soul departing, insofar as I have one."

"How surprising. If you're going to die anyway, isn't a fine assassination better than a slow, cancerous death?"

"You call this a fine assassination?"

"In the eyes of the assassin, murder is always beautiful. It's the victim who has cause for complaint. Right at this moment, are you really interested in the artistic value of your death? You must admit you aren't."

"I admit I'm not. Turn me over, I beg you."

The journalist grabbed hold of the mass by his hip and armpit and swung him over on his back, grunting with the effort. The fat man was breathing convulsively. It took several minutes for his terrorized face to regain a measure of serenity.

"So what is this thing that you have just discovered and that you are so eager to share with me?"

"I wanted to tell you: that was a rotten thing to have to go through."

"And then?"

"Isn't that enough?"

"What do you mean? Is that all you have to say? It has taken you eighty-three years to find out what everyone has known since birth?"

"Well you see, I didn't know. I had to be about to die to understand how horrible it is—not the death we all know nothing about, but the very instant of dying. It is a very rotten thing. Maybe other people have the necessary foresight, but I didn't."

"You're joking, aren't you?"

"No. Until today, I always thought that death was death, period. It was neither good nor bad, it was a disappearance. I didn't realize that there was a difference between that death and the moment of one's death, which is unbearable. Yes, it's very strange: I'm still not afraid of death, but from now on I will sweat with fear at the thought of what I'll have to go through, even if it only lasts a second."

"Are you ashamed, then?"

"Yes and no."

"Shit! Must I make you crawl again?"

"Let me explain. Yes, I am ashamed at the thought of having inflicted that passage upon Léopoldine. But I persist in believing, or at least hoping, that she was granted an exemption. The fact remains that I examined her face during her brief death throes, and I saw no anxiety there."

"What wonderful illusions you've found to ease your conscience."

"I don't give a damn about my conscience. My quest is on a higher level."

"Dear Lord."

"You said the word: yes, perhaps to certain exceptional human beings Our Lord allows a passage without suffering or anxiety, an ecstatic death. I think that Léopoldine was granted such a miracle."

"Listen, your story is already despicable enough as it is; do you want to make it even more grotesque by invoking God, ecstasy, and miracles? Perhaps you imagine you have perpetrated some sort of mystical murder?"

"Certainly."

"You are completely out to lunch. Do you want to know the reality of this mystical murder, you sick pervert? Do you know the first thing a body does after it dies? It pisses, Monsieur, and shits whatever remains in its intestines."

"You are repugnant. Cease your comedy, you're bothering me."

"I bother you, do I? Going around murdering people, that doesn't bother you, but the idea that one of your victims might piss and shit, that's intolerable, isn't it? And the water in your lake must have been very murky, when you went to fish out your cousin's corpse, if you didn't see the contents of her intestines rising to the surface."

"Hold your tongue, for pity's sake!"

"Pity for whom? For an assassin who is not even capable of assuming the biological consequences of his crime?"

"I swear to you, I swear to you that it didn't happen the way you say it did."

"Oh, really? So Léopoldine had neither bladder nor intestines?"

"Yes she did, but . . . it didn't happen the way you say it did."

"Let's just say, rather, that you can't stand the idea."

"The idea is unbearable, indeed, but it did not happen the way you say it did."

"Do you intend to go on repeating that until you die? You'd do better to explain."

"Alas, I cannot explain my conviction; however, I know that it did not happen the way you say it did."

"Do you know what they call this type of conviction? It is called autosuggestion."

"Mademoiselle, since I am unable to make myself understood, would you allow me to approach the question from a different angle?"

"Do you really believe there is a different angle?"

"I fear I do, yes."

"Well then, go ahead; we've gotten this far."

"Mademoiselle, have you ever loved someone?"

"I don't believe it! The lonely hearts column!"

"No, Mademoiselle. If you had ever loved someone, you would know that that has nothing to do with it. Poor Nina, you have never been in love."

"Don't talk about stuff like this with me, do you mind? And then don't call me Nina, it makes me uncomfortable."

"Why?"

"I don't know. There's something revolting about hearing my name said by an obese murderer."

"What a pity. And yet I really did want to call you Nina. What are you afraid of, Nina?"

"I'm not afraid of anything. You disgust me, that's all. And stop calling me Nina."

"What a pity. I need to call you something."

"Why?"

"My poor young lady, you are so hardened, so mature—but in some respects you are still like a newborn lamb. Don't you know it means, when a person needs to say a name? Do you imagine that I feel the same need for just anybody? Never, my child. If, deep within, one feels the desire to say a person's name, it is because one loves that person."

The journalist looked at him, speechless.

"Yes, Nina. I love you, Nina."

"Have you finished with this utter nonsense?"

"It's the truth, Nina. I had a first inkling of it a little while ago, and then I thought I had made a mistake, but I have not made a mistake. This, more than anything, is what I had to tell you when I was dying. I think I can no longer live without you, Nina. I love you."

"Wake up, imbecile."

"I have never been more lucid."

"Lucidity hardly becomes you."

"That doesn't matter. I no longer matter, I am all yours."

"Stop your raving, Monsieur Tach. I know very well that you don't love me. There is nothing about me that could possibly be to your liking."

"That is what I thought, too, Nina, but this love is far above all that."

"For pity's sake, don't tell me you love me for my soul, or I shall laugh so hard I'll cry."

"No, this love is greater still."

"I find you very ethereal, all of a sudden."

"Don't you understand that it is possible to love someone outside of any known reference?"

"No."

"That's a pity, Nina, and yet I do love you, with all the mystery the verb suggests."

"Stop it! Let me guess: you're looking for a decent ending for your novel, isn't that it?"

"If you only knew how I've lost interest in that novel over the last few minutes!"

"I don't believe it for a second. You are obsessed by the unfinished nature of it. You were disgusted upon learning that I have no personal connection with you, so now you're trying to fabricate a personal link from scratch, by inventing some last-minute love story. You have such a hatred of insignificance that you could make up the most enormous lies to give meaning to something that will never have any."

"You are wrong, Nina! Love has no meaning, and that is why it is sacred."

"Don't try to fool me with your rhetoric. You love no one, except for Léopoldine's corpse. You should be ashamed, moreover, to defile the only love of your life by saying such outlandish things to me."

"I am not defiling that love, on the contrary. By loving you, I am proving that Léopoldine taught me to love."

"Sophistry."

"It would be sophistry, if love did not obey rules that are completely estranged from those of logic."

"Listen, Monsieur Tach, you may go ahead and write such nonsense in your novel if it amuses you, but stopped using me as a guinea pig."

"Nina, it does not amuse me. Love is not for amusement. Love serves no purpose other than love."

"How thrilling."

"Indeed. If you could understand the meaning of the verb, you would be as thrilled as I am in this moment, Nina."

"Please spare me your thrill, would you? And stop calling me Nina, or I will no longer be able to answer for my acts."

"Do not answer for your acts, Nina. And let yourself be loved, since you cannot love me in return."

"Love you? That's all I need. I'd have to be a real pervert to be able to love you."

"So be a pervert, Nina, it would make me so happy."

"The thought of making you happy is utterly revolting. No one is less deserving of happiness than you are."

"I disagree."

"Of course you do."

"I may be horrible, ugly, and nasty, I can be the most vile person on the planet, and yet I do possess one very rare quality, a quality so fine that I no longer find myself unworthy."

"Let me guess: modesty?"

"No. My quality is that I am capable of love."

"And in the name of that sublime quality, you would like me to wash your feet with my tears and say, 'Prétextat, I love you'?"

"Say my name again, it feels so good."

"Be quiet, you make me want to puke."

"You are marvelous, Nina. You have an extraordinary personality, a fiery temperament cloaked in icy hardness. You are proud and bold. You have everything to make the perfect lover, if only you were capable of love."

"I should warn you that if you are taking me for the reincarnation of Léopoldine, you are mistaken. I have nothing in common with that ecstatic little girl."

"I know that. Have you ever known ecstasy, Nina?"

"I find your question utterly inappropriate."

"And it is. Everything is inappropriate in this matter, the love you inspire to start with. So, since we've gotten this far, Nina, do not hesitate to answer my question, which is more chaste than you might expect: have you ever known ecstasy, Nina?"

"I don't know. What I do know is that at the moment I feel no ecstasy."

"You do not know love, you do not know ecstasy: you know nothing. My little Nina, how can you cling to life the way you do, when you don't even know it?"

"Why are you saying such things? So that I'll be perfectly docile and let you kill me?"

"I will not kill you, Nina. Just now I thought I might, but in the meantime I have crawled, and the urge disappeared."

"I could die laughing. So you actually thought you could murder me, old and disabled as you are? I thought you were repulsive, but in fact, you are simply stupid."

"Love makes us stupid, it's a well-known fact, Nina."

"Oh please, spare me, don't talk to me anymore about your love, I can feel a sort of murderous urge welling up inside me."

"Is that possible? But, Nina, that's how it begins."

"The way what begins?"

"Love. Might I have shown you the way to ecstasy? I can't tell you how proud I am, Nina. The urge to kill has just died in me, and here it is reborn in you. You have just begun to live: are you aware of that?"

"All I'm aware of is the depth of my exasperation."

"I am witnessing the most extraordinary spectacle: like any ordinary person, I believed that reincarnation was a post-mortem phenomenon. And now before my very eyes, my very living eyes, I see you turning into me!"

"I have never received a more libelous insult!"

"The depth of your irritation is proof that your life has begun, Nina. Henceforth, you will always be as furious as I have been, you will be allergic to bad faith, you will explode with imprecations and ecstasy, you will be inspired, you will revel in your anger and fear nothing."

"Have you finished, you bloated boil?"

"You know that I am right."

"Absolutely not! I am not you."

"Not yet completely, but it won't take long."

"What do you mean?"

"You'll find out soon enough. It's remarkable. The things I say come to pass before my very eyes, as I am saying them. I have become the prophet of the present—not the future, the present, do you understand?"

"I understand that you have lost your mind."

"You are the one who has taken it, as you will take all the rest. Nina, I have never known such ecstasy!"

"Where are your tranquilizers?"

"Nina, I will have all eternity to be tranquil, once you kill me."

"What are you saying?"

"Let me speak. What I have to say is too important. Whether you want to or not, you are becoming my avatar. With each metamorphosis of my being, an individual worthy of love was waiting: the first time, it was Léopoldine, and I'm the one who killed her; and now it's you, and you will kill me. That is fair enough, don't you think? I am so happy that it is you: thanks to me, you are about to discover what love is."

"Thanks to you, I am about to discover what consternation is."

"You see? You said so yourself. Love begins with consternation."

"Just now you said it began with a desire for murder."

"It's the same thing. Listen to what is welling up inside you, Nina: feel that immense astonishment. Have you ever heard a better-constructed symphony? The workings of it are too perfect and too subtle for others to perceive. Have you noticed the amazing diversity of instruments? Their incongruous chords should create only cacophony—and yet, Nina, have you ever heard anything more beautiful? Dozens of movements are being superimposed through you, making your skull a cathedral, your body a vague and infinite sound box, your thin flesh a trance, all causing your cartilage to relax: you have been possessed by that which is unnamable."

Silence. The journalist threw her head back.

"Your skull feels heavy, doesn't it? I know what it is. You will see that you'll never get used to it."

"To what?"

"To the unnamable. Try to lift your head, Nina, however heavy your skull might be, and look at me."

The creature did as he asked, with an effort.

"You must concede that despite the inconvenience, it is divinely pleasant. I'm very pleased that you have understood at last. Try to imagine now what Léopoldine's death was like. Just now, the instant of my death seemed intolerable because I was crawling, in both senses of the term. But to go from life to death in a moment of ecstasy is a mere formality. Why? Because in such moments one does not know whether one is dead or alive. It would be inexact to say that my cousin died without suffering or without realizing it, like someone dying in their sleep: the truth is that she died without dying, because she was already no longer alive."

"Careful now, what you just said stinks of Tachian rhetoric."

"And what you are feeling, is that Tachian rhetoric, Nina? Look at me, my charming little avatar. You will have to get used to scorning other people's logic from now on. Consequently, you will have to get used to being alone—don't regret it."

"I'll miss you."

"It's very kind of you to say that."

"You know very well that kindness has nothing to do with any of this."

"Don't worry, you will see me again at every moment of ecstasy."

"Will it happen often?"

"To be honest, I had not experienced ecstasy for sixty-five and a half years, but the ecstasy I am feeling at the moment erases all the lost time as if it had never existed. You will also have to get used to ignoring the calendar."

"What next."

"Do not be sad, dear avatar. Do not forget that I love you. And love is eternal, as you well know."

"Do you know that, coming from a Nobel laureate, there is something irresistibly delicious about such platitudes?"

"You don't know how right you are. When you have attained my degree of sophistication, you do not dare say anything terribly ordinary without disfiguring it, without giving it a touch of the strangest of paradoxes. How many writers have taken up this career with the sole purpose of, some day, reaching a place beyond banality, a sort of no man's land where words are always virginal. Perhaps that's what immaculate conception is: to say the words that are a hair's breadth away from bad taste, yet still retain a sort of miraculous state of grace, always above the crowd, above any ridiculous grumbling. I am the last individual on earth who can say 'I love you' without being obscene. You are very lucky indeed."

"Lucky? Is it not rather a curse?"

"Lucky, Nina. Do you realize, without me, your life would have been so terribly boring!"

"What do you know?"

"It stands out a mile. Did you not say yourself that you were a dirty little muckraker? In the long term, you would have wearied of that. Sooner or later, you have to stop being interested in other people's shit, and begin to create your own. Without me, you would never have been able to. Henceforth, oh avatar, you will have access to the divine initiatives of creators."

"I do feel a troubling initiative stirring in me."

"That's normal. Doubt and fear are the accessories of great initiatives. You will gradually come to understand that your anxiety is part of the pleasure. And you need pleasure, Nina, don't you? Clearly I've taught you everything and brought you everything. Love, for a start: darling avatar, I tremble at the thought that without me you would never have known what love is. A few minutes ago we were talking about verbs without an imperative: do you know that the verb 'to love' presents similar deficiencies?"

"Now what are you going on about?"

"It is only conjugated in the singular. Its plural forms are never anything other than disguised singulars."

"That's your point of view."

"Not at all: have I not proven that when two people love each other, one of the two has to disappear to restore the singular—hence, no imperative?"

"Don't tell me that you killed Léopoldine to comply with some grammatical ideal?"

"Does the cause seem so very futile to you? Do you know of a more imperious need than conjugation? I would have you know, little avatar, that if conjugation did not exist, we would not even be aware of being distinct individuals, and this sublime conversation would be impossible."

"If only."

"Come now, do not disdain your own pleasure."

"My pleasure? There is not a jot of pleasure in me, and I feel nothing, other than a terrible desire to strangle you."

"Well, well, you've taken your time, my dear avatar. I have spent at least ten minutes, with exemplary transparency, trying to get you to make your mind up. I've exasperated you, I've pushed you to the limit to tear away your last scruples, and still you haven't gone through with it. What are you waiting for, my tender love?"

"I find it hard to believe that it's what you really want."

"I give you my word."

"And besides, I'm not in the habit . . . "

"It will come."

"I'm afraid."

"So much the better."

"And what if I don't do it?"

"The atmosphere will become unbearable. Believe me, we've gotten this far, you no longer have any choice. Besides, you are offering me the unique opportunity of dying in the same conditions as Léopoldine: at last I will know what she went through. Go to it, avatar, I am ripe."

The journalist did as he asked, flawlessly. It was quick and clean. Classicism never commits any errors of taste.

When it was done, Nina switched off the tape recorder and sat down in the middle of the sofa. She was very calm. If she began talking to herself, it was not the effect of some mental disturbance. She spoke the way one speaks to a close friend, with a somewhat mirthful tenderness: "You mad old fool, you almost had me there. Your words annoyed me beyond belief; I was on the verge of losing my mind. Now I feel much better. I have to confess that you were right: strangling is a very pleasant rite."

And the avatar gazed admiringly at her hands.

The paths that lead to God are impenetrable. More impenetrable still are those that lead to success. In the wake of this incident, there was a veritable stampede for the works of Prétextat Tach. Ten years later, he was a classic.

About the Author

Amélie Nothomb is the author of over twenty novels, including *Tokyo Fiancée*, published by Europa Editions in 2009. Nothomb's books have been translated into over fifteen languages and have been awarded the French Academy's 1999 Grand Prix for the Novel, the René-Fallet prize, the Alain-Fournier prize, and the Grand Prix Giono in 2008. Nothomb lives in Paris and Brussels.

Carmine Abate
Between Two Seas
"A moving portrayal of generational continuity."
—*Kirkus*
224 pp • $14.95 • 978-1-933372-40-2

Salwa Al Neimi
The Proof of the Honey
"Al Neimi announces the end of a taboo in the Arab world:
that of *sex!*"
—*Reuters*
144 pp • $15.00 • 978-1-933372-68-6

Alberto Angela
A Day in the Life of Ancient Rome
"Fascinating and accessible."
—*Il Giornale*
392 pp • $16.00 • 978-1-933372-71-6

Muriel Barbery
The Elegance of the Hedgehog
"Gently satirical, exceptionally winning and inevitably bittersweet."
—Michael Dirda, *The Washington Post*
336 pp • $15.00 • 978-1-933372-60-0

Gourmet Rhapsody
"In the pages of this book, Barbery shows off her finest gift: lightness."
—*La Repubblica*
176 pp • $15.00 • 978-1-933372-95-2

Stefano Benni
Margherita Dolce Vita
"A modern fable...hilarious social commentary."—*People*
240 pp • $14.95 • 978-1-933372-20-4

Timeskipper
"Benni again unveils his Italian brand of magical realism."
—*Library Journal*
400 pp • $16.95 • 978-1-933372-44-0

Romano Bilenchi
The Chill
120 pp • $15.00 • 978-1-933372-90-7

Massimo Carlotto
The Goodbye Kiss
"A masterpiece of Italian noir."
—*Globe and Mail*
160 pp • $14.95 • 978-1-933372-05-1

Death's Dark Abyss
"A remarkable study of corruption and redemption."
—*Kirkus* (starred review)
160 pp • $14.95 • 978-1-933372-18-1

The Fugitive
"[Carlotto is] the reigning king of Mediterranean noir."
—*The Boston Phoenix*
176 pp • $14.95 • 978-1-933372-25-9

(with Marco Videtta)
Poisonville
"The business world as described by Carlotto and Videtta
in *Poisonville* is frightening as hell."
—*La Repubblica*
224 pp • $15.00 • 978-1-933372-91-4

Francisco Coloane
Tierra del Fuego
"Coloane is the Jack London of our times."—Alvaro Mutis
192 pp • $14.95 • 978-1-933372-63-1

Giancarlo De Cataldo
The Father and the Foreigner
"A slim but touching noir novel from one of Italy's best writers
in the genre."—*Quaderni Noir*
144 pp • $15.00 • 978-1-933372-72-3

Shashi Deshpande
The Dark Holds No Terrors
"[Deshpande is] an extremely talented storyteller."—*Hindustan Times*
272 pp • $15.00 • 978-1-933372-67-9

Helmut Dubiel
Deep in the Brain: Living with Parkinson's Disease
"A book that begs reflection."—*Die Zeit*
144 pp • $15.00 • 978-1-933372-70-9

Steve Erickson
Zeroville
"A funny, disturbing, daring and demanding novel—Erickson's best."
—*The New York Times Book Review*
352 pp • $14.95 • 978-1-933372-39-6

Elena Ferrante
The Days of Abandonment
"The raging, torrential voice of [this] author is something rare."
—*The New York Times*
192 pp • $14.95 • 978-1-933372-00-6

Troubling Love
"Ferrante's polished language belies the rawness of her imagery."
—*The New Yorker*
144 pp • $14.95 • 978-1-933372-16-7

The Lost Daughter
"So refined, almost translucent."—*The Boston Globe*
144 pp • $14.95 • 978-1-933372-42-6

Jane Gardam
Old Filth
"Old Filth belongs in the Dickensian pantheon of memorable characters."
—*The New York Times Book Review*
304 pp • $14.95 • 978-1-933372-13-6

The Queen of the Tambourine
"A truly superb and moving novel."—*The Boston Globe*
272 pp • $14.95 • 978-1-933372-36-5

The People on Privilege Hill
"Engrossing stories of hilarity and heartbreak."—*Seattle Times*
208 pp • $15.95 • 978-1-933372-56-3

The Man in the Wooden Hat
"Here is a writer who delivers the world we live in…with memorable and moving skill."—*The Boston Globe*
240 pp • $15.00 • 978-1-933372-89-1

Alicia Giménez-Bartlett
Dog Day
"Delicado and Garzón prove to be one of the more engaging sleuth teams to debut in a long time."—*The Washington Post*
320 pp • $14.95 • 978-1-933372-14-3

Prime Time Suspect
"A gripping police procedural."—*The Washington Post*
320 pp • $14.95 • 978-1-933372-31-0

Death Rites
"Petra is developing into a good cop, and her earnest efforts to assert her authority…are worth cheering."—*The New York Times*
304 pp • $16.95 • 978-1-933372-54-9

Katharina Hacker
The Have-Nots
"Hacker's prose soars."—*Publishers Weekly*
352 pp • $14.95 • 978-1-933372-41-9

Patrick Hamilton
Hangover Square
"Patrick Hamilton's novels are dark tunnels of misery, loneliness, deceit, and sexual obsession."—*New York Review of Books*
336 pp • $14.95 • 978-1-933372-06-

James Hamilton-Paterson
Cooking with Fernet Branca
"Irresistible!"—*The Washington Post*
288 pp • $14.95 • 978-1-933372-01-3

Amazing Disgrace
"It's loads of fun, light and dazzling as a peacock feather."
—*New York Magazine*
352 pp • $14.95 • 978-1-933372-19-8

Rancid Pansies
"Campy comic saga about hack writer and self-styled 'culinary genius' Gerald Samper."—*Seattle Times*
288 pp • $15.95 • 978-1-933372-62-4

Seven-Tenths: The Sea and Its Thresholds
"The kind of book that, were he alive now, Shelley might have written."
—*Charles Spawson*
416 pp • $16.00 • 978-1-933372-69-3

Alfred Hayes
The Girl on the Via Flaminia
"Immensely readable."—*The New York Times*
164 pp • $14.95 • 978-1-933372-24-2